In memory of my mother, Barbara Jean,
who loved *Maud: A Garden Tale*
1924-2020

# A SOLEMN CURFEW

## AND OTHER DARK TALES

BY

# BEV ALLEN

CATHAVEN
PRESS

# A SOLEMN CURFEW

## AND OTHER DARK TALES

**ISBN: 978-1-9160212-5-9**

Publishers: Dave Brzeski and Jilly Paddock (as Cathaven Press)
Editing/Interior design: Dave Brzeski and Jilly Paddock
Editorial Assistance/Introduction: John Linwood Grant

'*A Solemn Curfew*' originally appeared in *The Secrets of Castle Drakon* (Thorstruck Press 2014)
'*Maud: A Garden Tale*' originally appeared in *Pulp Idol* (SFX 2007)
'*Cunning Water*' originally appeared in *Darkness Abound* (Migla Press 2016)
All other stories first appeared in the original, self-published ebook version of this collection, with the exception of '*No Sure Foundation*', which is original to this edition.

Published by
Cathaven Press,
Peterborough,
United Kingdom
cathaven.press@cathaven.co.uk

# INTRODUCTION

It's a pleasure to be able to introduce this book, *A Solemn Curfew*, because the truth is that Bev Allen's strange fiction is rather underrated — perhaps because she herself has never made any great fuss about it. Yet over the years, she has cunningly created a modest number of stories which straddle what is now called Folk Horror, and the general realm of supernatural tales, both period-set and contemporary. To have them collected together here is a delight.

There are perhaps two particular aspects which distinguish her stories, and make it well worth your while to read this book. The first is that Allen captures a certain fabulous quality, by which I mean a touch of classic fables, and offers the underlying tone, the sensation, of an old, old story in a framework which is no longer stiff or predictable. This is a tradition with a certain wry humour, and also an almost casual violence — '*The Girl in the Water*' and '*Swansong*', for example, cover very unpleasant subjects at the same time as being written with style. She herself has said of her stories:

*"...They all have their roots in English folklore and in the sort of tales that were told around the fire to stop people thinking about what might be lurking in the dark. I love folk music and folk songs, I adore Morris dancing and the guys who dance with stag's horns. I like the so-called Holy Wells and hill forts and stone circles. I love the roots of England and the history deep in its bones. And I like to put just a small twist in the mix."*

Even in Allen's contemporary world, there are no real boundaries between modern life and the Wildwoods. If pagan water spirits and Hidden Folk exist, they exist alongside that dreadful wallpaper and the tasteless garden border, in the suburban semi-detached and the rented room. She offers that continuity where Kipling's Puck or Shakepeare's Ariel might toy and conjure with the electric kettle — but in Allen's interpretation, they might well be ready to electrocute the lot of us with it. 'Maud: A Garden Tale' demonstrates the endurance of the "old things" only too clearly, with her trademark directness.

And 'Maud' also exemplifies the second aspect of Allen's work which makes it noteworthy. Still in keeping with their "roots", these are stories with appetites and needs — food and fertilisation, compost and copulation, abound. Found in earth and water are the secrets of Life and Death, not as vague, spiritual concepts, but as natural hungers and desires. This is a very "soil-under-the-fingernails" book, as might be written by a slightly deranged gardener, and Allen's own interests in cooking and the history of food often shine through, emerging especially in tales such as 'A Solemn Curfew' itself and 'Say Cheese'. These are stories you can *feel*, not airy narrations; the humour is often dark and deadpan, and the better for it. You know that Allen has a wicked mind.

In short, *A Solemn Curfew and Other Dark Tales* is a clever (and subtly worrying) read. It skilfully blends elements of folklore, Folk Horror, and British unease — and I doubt you will be disappointed by digging into it.

*John Linwood Grant*
*Yorkshire, April 2022*

# CUNNING WATER

*"Trust not those cunning waters..."*
Shakespeare, *King John*

It was time for the first daily act of devotion.

Piously Brenda donned the appropriate garments, armed herself with the correct accoutrements and approached the holy of holies with the same feelings of reverence she experienced every day. Her chagrin knew no bounds when she beheld the scene before her. Sacrilege had been done here in this hallowed place.

Desecration abounded; it was bad enough Kevin left wet towels all over the floor, but there was also pee up the back of the toilet and yes... it was so gross... there was a disgusting tell-tale brown streak on the inside of the bowl. She turned to see what he had wrought in the shower cubicle and all her fears were confirmed; there was water dripping and he had left an open bottle of gel on the shelf.

It was going to take hours to return the

bathroom suite (Aphrodite: pattern two: snow white) to its pristine purity. There were limescale stains on all the taps (Arcadian Rain Splash) and she would have to wipe all the tiles (white with a hint of grey) before tackling the floor (Italian marble pattern). She snapped her rubber gloves into position and began.

From the bathroom she went to the bedroom to collect some clothes for washing. It did not have the same power to please her as the bathroom. Kevin had insisted they buy the Florida Chic bed, when Brenda would have preferred a futon. She curled her lip at the king-sized monstrosity, only slightly redeemed in her eyes by the white duvet cover with embroidered white detail, matching pillows, cushions and throw.

Downstairs in the through lounge everything was shades of pale grey and white, except for one statement wall which was papered with a leaf motif. Brenda had echoed this on the mantelpiece over the "living" flame fire with a "statement" glass vase holding a single stem of leaves. Not real ones of course; they might have dropped and soiled the pale solid wood floors.

A light dusting and a quick once-over with a mop would return the room to Brenda's idea of comfort, but it could wait. There were more important matters in the kitchen.

One look was enough to tell her Kevin's fell hand had fallen here; toast crumbs all over the counter and a dirty coffee mug just left in the sink with a knife coated in butter and marmalade. She looked in the fridge. Yes, there were crumbs in the butter again.

If she was truthful, something Brenda prided herself upon, but was in fact remarkably allergic to, she liked the way Kevin left things. She loved to clean, and bringing the kitchen, with its shining work tops (white granite), stainless steel appliances and units (piano black), back to detritus and fingerprint free perfection, it was just gravy on her mash, or it would have been if Brenda had allowed anything with such potential to sully anywhere near the cooker.

She was not as displeased as might have been expected. Disciplining Kevin over the state of the knife, the butter and the counter would do admirably for this evening's conversation. She allowed herself a second cup of coffee from one of her favourite mugs (white with an eau-de-nil design) and reflected upon Kevin and the garden.

He was being very difficult over the garden.

She sometimes wondered why she had married him. It was true there had not been that many offers or opportunities, not with her having to look after mother until the end, but she did wonder if she could have done better. She had made up her mind when his promotion at work coincided with her mother finally getting the hint and joining her father in the corporation cemetery. The sale of the old house and the moderate mortgage Kevin was then able to support made her accept. He could now offer her the one thing she had always wanted, a home free from the touch of another woman.

It had always revolted her, cooking in a place where another woman had cooked and, even worse, bathing somewhere another had bathed. Before she married, no amount of cleaning could quite reconcile her to sharing all the facilities with her mother. Her memories of her father were vague, but never failed to cause a shudder.

It had not been hard persuading Kevin they should buy a new build on a greenfield site. There had been financial incentives which appealed to him and as she was providing the bulk of the money, he had not hesitated or tried to talk her into something closer to the town. It had meant a longer commute for him, but there had been enough money to provide him with a new car and the house came with a garage to put it in, so any qualms he might have felt were easily dispelled.

The choice of fixtures and fitting had been a little harder. He had wanted to bring a great deal of clutter and rubbish with him into the marriage. Brenda had quickly put a stop to that idea, as she told him it was hardly fair as she was not going to bring anything from her old home. She did not tell him that given the chance she would have cheerfully consigned the whole lot to the fire.

He had had some odd idea he was going to have some say in colour scheme and fixtures as well, but she forestalled any arguments over the look of their house by going to the builders without him and picking out exactly what she wanted.

The only real problem up until now had been the bed, but in time she was sure she could rectify that blot on her landscape. At the moment a far more important blot was confronting her, the back garden of 27, Water Meadow Row.

When they had chosen their plot from the plans the builder offered them, Brenda had made sure they got one of the ones at the bottom of the slope.

It meant they would have no neighbours behind them. Beyond their boundary there was nothing but more slope ending in a narrow ditch; the land across from it on the other side was designated as agricultural use only. She had done some checking on this; the last thing she wanted was the smell of cows or pigs wafting up over the fence, but it appeared it was for sheep and hay. Brenda, in her innocence, thought there was something nice and clean about sheep, all that soft wool and frisky lambs. She also thought hay was something which was secured in ricks, so that was all right as well.

Even so, she had made sure the fence which surrounded the property was reasonably high and made of solid panelling just in case. Kevin had got uncharacteristically excited by the fencing and talked about climbing roses, clematis and honeysuckle.

Brenda had been unaware of these latent horticultural traits until then and saw curbing them was going to require some thought. She had her own ideas of the perfect garden and they involved the elimination of earth, not the introduction of things which required it.

The trouble with earth was it was brown and Brenda had never liked things that were brown. To her brown equalled dirt and all dirt was, by and large brown, therefore its removal or concealment was one of her main concerns.

In her garden scheme half the ground would disappear under decking, a portion of what remained would be paved for a patio and what was left she would allow Kevin to lay to lawn. Mowing it would give him something to do each weekend after he had cleaned the car.

There would be no flower beds. If Kevin, who had mentioned a vegetable patch, wished to indulge in such things, he could do so in a few pots where dirt could be contained and hidden from view.

She carefully washed up her coffee mug and the spoon she had used, dried them and put them away; then she wiped down the sink, making sure she dried and polished it, the taps and the draining board. Advising Kevin what she had decided to do in the garden would have to be tackled carefully; he had proved to be unreasonably stubborn over some matters. She opened one of the doors of the stainless steel double size fridge-freezer and surveyed the neatly packed shelves.

Was this going to be a problem which would require her to use the cooker? So far she had avoided dirtying the oven, but had been forced to use the hob to heat up the occasional tin of soup. There was a frozen pie on one shelf; this at least could be cooked in the free-standing halogen oven. Brenda loved that oven, it was so easy to keep clean.

There were also some frozen mashed potatoes — such a boon — doing away with touching the brown tubers so often coated in dirt, and a pack of peas. Pie, mash and peas would soften him up and he could have arctic roll for pudding if he showed signs of needing any more persuasion.

Later, as she lay under the white duvet listening to Kevin snore, she wondered how much longer she would be able to endure the relationship. The pie, mash and peas had worked as far as the decking was concerned and the arctic roll had done the trick with the lawn, but she had not been able to win him over on the subject of a paved patio.

He wanted some flower beds and worse of all, he wanted a pond. Brenda shuddered at the idea of a pond, a pool of stagnant water just yards away from her back door. The idea disturbed her so much she even considered resorting to sex to make him change his mind.

Sex had been a disappointment to Brenda. She had always been curious about it and read any number of books which alluded to the subject. They had all made it sound very alluring and she had almost been looking forward to trying it. What none of the authors had mentioned was the amount of liquid involved, all that leakage and sweat and stickiness. She shuddered again. Kevin would have to have his pond, at least for a while.

In the end the flower beds were not as bad as Brenda had feared, as Kevin was very keen on something called weed-suppressing mulch. She had gone to the garden centre with him and by a few carefully chosen words had steered him away from cocoa husk — Brenda had never liked chocolate, far too brown to be nice no matter what anyone said — and peat, and towards slate chippings. She used an environmental argument she had once overheard on the radio.

As she gazed out of the kitchen window at the miniature maple tree standing alone in its bed surrounded by some herbaceous plant covered in small white flowers, she thought how charming the surround of grey flakes made the picture. She acknowledged she might possibly have been wrong about flower beds, provided they did not expand.

What she was not reconciled to was the pond. She had gone out the weekend Kevin had dug the hole for it. It had been a mistake, because she came home to filthy muddy foot prints all over the kitchen floor. They even trailed across the wood floor of the hall, up the stairs and into the bathroom. What she found in the shower tray kept her awake for three nights running. As she lay, unable to sleep with the rage boiling inside her, her mind's eye alternated between the sediment in the shower and the pile of black rubber fabric which was draped over half the garden.

Kevin told her it was just the pond liner and when he had fed it all into the hole and trimmed it back she would not see it. He had been true to his word, it had gone and the edge of the pond was now a ring of round stones, but every time Brenda looked all she could see was the black filled gouge in the ground now filled with dirty water. Apparently, it would settle down in time and, with the addition of a few oxygenating plants, the water would become as clear as the stuff which came out of the tap. It would, Kevin told her, reflect the sky and the branches of the maple, and attract wildlife, which was not something Brenda wished to hear. Wildlife was, by and large brown and frequently filthy in its habits.

As autumn turned the leaves of the small maple tree blood red, the pond remained a dark spot on the garden. Every time Brenda looked out of the window to make sure no moss or lichen was making its home on the decking and no unwanted bird had disturbed the grey slate mulch, it seemed to mock her, a dark gleaming disc of irregularity. It did not even have the tact to be a perfect circle or oval. Kevin said he wanted it to look natural, Brenda wanted it to look gone.

\* \* \*

Shopping was not something Brenda enjoyed doing; she took no pleasure in the purchase of clothes and shoes and she did not approve of the sort of knick-knacks which cluttered other people's homes, and she certainly had no time for books which were, in her opinion, neither decorative, nor useful, and gathered dust. Food had to be purchased and so did cleaning materials, but Brenda, who had never been able to master the art of word processing, took to online shopping like a duck to water. This all meant time was not wasted away from the home which needed her to keep it clean and tidy, so it was annoying to be forced into town on an errand for Kevin. He had forgotten to collect his dry cleaning and there was some sort of meeting the following day which required his best suit.

Everything might have been well if she had not been accosted by Mavis. Brenda had not seen the woman since her mother become too ill for visitors, or Brenda had been able with a reasonably clear conscience to say she was too ill for visitors. Up until then Mavis had been a regular on their doorstep.

She and Brenda`s mother would spend hours gossiping, drinking endless cups of tea and eating chocolate digestives. Brenda found the very thought of those two-tone brown circles repellent.

"Haven't seen you in an age, Bren," she said by way of greeting. "Not since you sold the old place and married what's-his-name."

"Kevin," Brenda supplied.

"That's the one." Mavis agreed. "How are things?"

It was hard to resist the temptation to boast and Brenda did not even make the attempt. Unfortunately it backfired on her, and before she could think of a reason to get out of it, she found she had extended Mavis an invitation to visit Number 27 and view for herself the perfection that was now Brenda's life.

Mavis lost no time in taking up the offer and was settling herself down on Brenda's sofa (Pandora pattern, oatmeal, with the optional Teflon coating) within the week. Her inquisitive eyes took in everything as they ranged about the room.

"Very nice," she said, with total insincerity. "But you could do with a bit of colour."

Brenda ignored this and set the tea tray down on the coffee table (white oak) and began to pour light golden tea into a white cups and saucers. She knew Mavis would have preferred a more mahogany brew, but she was not going to get it.

"And I'd get some carpet down on these floor boards if I was you. A nice shag pile would be good."

Brenda smiled and offered a plate of macaroons — she did not care for them herself, but there was a shop in town which made them and you could choose which colours you wanted. Mavis looked suspiciously at the pale lemon, pale pink, pale green and very, very pale mauve examples offered for her pleasure.

"I don't suppose you've got any chocolate digestives?"

"No," Brenda replied.

Mavis selected one of the pink macaroons and after an investigative sniff and an experimental nibble, stuffed the whole into her mouth and washed it down with a mouthful of tea.

"Not bad," she said, and began to work her way through the whole plate.

The conversation ranged over a number of subjects, but its main purpose was for Mavis to discover just how much Brenda's mother had left her, how much she had sold the old house for and how much Kevin was earning. The last macaroon disappeared and Brenda showed no signs of producing more, nor had she been forthcoming on any of the things Mavis was interested in, so she tried a change of tack.

"I was surprised when the council agreed to these houses being built here," she said.

"Why?"

"On account of the bourne."

"What is a bourne?" Brenda asked.

"It's a river," Mavis replied, well pleased with her ignorance. "One that only runs sometimes. In fact, it can disappear for years and years and years, then something happens and before you know it you can be thigh-deep in water."

"There is no river anywhere near here," Brenda replied.

Mavis laughed.

"Bless you, dearie," she said. "It's just behind that fence of yours."

She settled herself more comfortably into the sofa.

"These days it just looks all dried up, but my granny used to tell me how they would bring the horse down to drink when she was a little girl."

Brenda looked unimpressed, so she added, "And when the circus came to visit it was so deep the elephants had a bath in there."

The bombshell failed to detonate.

"That was a very long time ago," Brenda said. "I hardly think the council would have granted planning permission if there was the remotest chance of that ditch ever having more than a trickle of water in it again."

"You mustn't call it a ditch." Mavis warned. "It's a bourne and bournes are special. Especially that bourne."

She carried on for some time on this theme, the water getting deeper and deeper as she recalled all the stories her granny and great granny had told her and when these failed to impress she hinted at the "special" nature of bournes, things ordinary people did not understand and would be best to avoid.

When this also failed to produce the result she wanted, she snapped.

"You better watch out, one good shower of rain and you could find yourself stuck upstairs waiting for the fire brigade to come and get you in a boat."

Brenda congratulated herself on failing to provide chocolate digestives and inquired if her visitor would like to use the facilities before she left, despite knowing she would be forced to clean the whole bathroom from top to bottom afterwards.

Mavis took more umbrage and treated herself to a nose around the bedrooms before she left. Her information about the bourne had not had the effect she had hoped it would; offering succour and comfort to the distressed was one of her favourite hobbies and Brenda had robbed her of the chance to enjoy herself.

She tried one last throw of the dice as she left,

"I do hope everything works out for you, dearie. People really shouldn't interfere with the old places and the old ways, it always comes out badly in the end."

It fell upon deaf ears. If the old ways meant shag pile carpets, brown beverages and browner biscuits, Brenda was more than happy to leave them alone.

* * *

The maple shed its leaves and suffered a setback in Brenda's good opinion; every day she was forced to go out and collect them to stop them blowing around and making the whole place look untidy. Kevin said something about a compost bin and Brenda put her foot down. All rubbish would go in the dustbin where it belonged. He did not argue, not that time.

The real row came in the spring. Winter had alternated between rain and cold and there had been a mercifully brief flurry of snow. Brenda thought snow perfectly lovely when it came down and when it lay undisturbed, all white and pristine, but the slush and filthy foot prints which came later were an anathema and as if things were not bad enough, when she went out in the garden to inspect the crocuses Kevin had planted the previous year she found the pond not looking dark and still, but a mass of grey slime.

Closer inspection proved it to be frogspawn and Brenda nearly fainted in horror. The second Kevin walked through the door she told him to get rid of it, every bit. The thought of all the wriggling black tadpoles which would result and worse, the frogs which would follow nearly sent her into hysterics, but instead of doing as he was told, Kevin said he would do no such thing, that he liked frogs and hoped there would be dozens and dozens of them.

She could not believe her ears and told him the pond would have to go as well. He told her that far from going the pond was going to have an extension. He was going to dig up some of the grass and make a bog garden.

It was probably the word "bog" which sent Brenda over the edge, everything the word conjured up, mud, dirt and smell, all of it. In the end Kevin moved into the spare room and as soon as she could Brenda had the Florida Chic bed moved in there with him and bought herself a futon.

This was possibly a mistake as it was the most uncomfortable thing she had ever slept on, but there was a principle to maintain. She still cleaned the house and cooked for him, as she was not having him dirty the kitchen with curry and pizzas, but they did not speak.

If she hoped the silent treatment would bring him to his senses she was wrong, but as she was not going to be the first to break it, she was forced to watch him dig and plant his bog garden. This time there was no decent grey slate mulch, she was forced to look at naked brown earth.

Kevin spent a great deal of time out in the garden after this. The bog seemed to be growing and he was forever doing things in the pond. It rained a lot, but this did not seem to bother him. He stayed out there despite the weather and dripped all over the floors when he did come inside.

Brenda could not understand what he found to do out there; often he did not come inside until it was dark. She worried away at the problem for weeks until she finally went looking for answers on the internet and the truth came to her in a blinding flash – he was having an affair! He was not in the garden at all, he was sneaking away to be with some woman.

All the girls on the website agreed and most of them had some very definite ideas about what she should do about it, and what she should do to the home-wrecking slut who had seduced him away from a good and loving wife.

Finding out who was keeping Kevin out in the garden was the first thing on Brenda's to do list. She had a few candidates, and first there was the suicide blonde next door. Not only did she dye her hair the most improbable shade of gilt, she also had no shame about hanging out her smalls on the line for the whole world to see. The sight of the leopard skin thong and matching uplift bra had been enough to send Brenda to knock on her door and protest. The woman had just laughed and closed the door. The second time she went to protest was over what Kevin told her were crotchless knickers — she had been told to go away, but not in those words.

As the summer approached Kevin spent even more time in the garden, not coming indoors until Brenda had gone to bed, but now she knew what she was looking for, she would go upstairs, pretend to get ready for bed, turn out the light and then creep downstairs again to watch where he went.

It was not easy; when the house lights were out there was very little illumination. There were no streetlights and because there were only open fields behind, the only light came from the stars or the moon when it was out. This was, however, enough to tell Brenda that whatever else Kevin was doing, he was not doing it away from home.

If there was someone else, they were out there with him; she could see the outline of a figure, a darker shade amid the shadows. She had no clue as to who it was, or even if it was a woman, but one thing was sure, it was not her-next-door, as even the smallest light would have lit that hair up like a neon sign.

He did seem to be talking to someone. She could hear the soft sound of what she thought were voices coming from over by the pond, but it might just have been the sound of Kevin playing with the water, a disgusting habit he had acquired. She even heard him laugh at one point. She could not remember the last time Kevin had laughed, she was not entirely sure she had ever heard him laugh.

Checking on Kevin's nightly garden activities became routine, but try as she might, she never managed to see who he was talking to. One evening she was fairly certain she saw him standing in the pond, actually standing in the water with his trouser legs rolled up to his knees. She had no idea what could possibly have motivated such behaviour — perhaps he was planting something. He need not think she was going to wash those trousers; he would have to have them dry cleaned before they came back into the house.

Her internet advisors told her she needed to get as much evidence as she could, anything which might assist in the divorce. Brenda had no intention of divorcing Kevin, as divorce was just the sort of messy situation which appalled her, but she thought she might find some weapon she could apply to the subject of ponds and more especially bogs. She was sure if she could get the garden back to the state she had wanted in the first place Kevin would improve and they could go back to sharing a room and a bed, and she could quietly dispose of the futon.

Perhaps the answer lay in the pond itself. She had not ventured out of the back door in months and she had not inspected the garden in daylight during that time either. Kevin slept in the back room, so she had not been able to even look down on it, but the morning after she heard, or thought she heard the laughter she went to his room once he had gone to work so she could inspect it from a safe distance.

The smell assaulted her nostrils like a fetid rat sliding up a greasy sewer pipe. The place was rank with the noisome odour of bed linen unchanged for weeks, socks left to fester, dust and that indefinable smell of Kevin, the one she evicted with air freshener wherever she found it.

Gagging, she cut a trail through the unwashed underpants to the window and took her first panoramic view of the garden in ages.

Beyond the fence the ditch was has it always had been, nothing more than a slightly greener dip in the landscape separating the housing estate from the fields. She noted the presence of cows in the field, but before she could fully embrace the awfulness of this, a far greater horror hit her between her unplucked eyebrows — Kevin had been empire building while he had been out in the garden!

The pond was twice the size it had been and judging by the growth around it, the bog had expanded as well. Even from this distance Brenda could see things she thought must be reeds and water lilies.

She raced down the stairs and out onto the decking. It was June now and the warm air should have been dry, but here in the garden it felt lush and damp and yet another smell went wriggling up Brenda's nose to slam dunk information, a thick, invading combination of verdant growth, vegetation rotting down to enrich soil already abundant with organic matter and of water, trickling, bubbling, seeping water.

Stepping off the decking onto what should have been grass, Brenda felt her feet sink. She looked down and instead of nice neat stems of thin leaf, she saw she was standing on deep sphagnum moss which oozed out water with every pressure. For a moment she was rooted to the spot, then a blue dragonfly flashed before her eyes and she screamed and ran back indoors.

He had turned the garden into a swamp!

For a while all she could do was sit at the kitchen table in shock. Who had encouraged him to do this dreadful thing? If it was not the thong woman who could it be? Was it the very odd woman who lived opposite, the one who owned the cats?

Cats were one of the many things Brenda would have liked controlled by environmental health. When they had first moved in the drive in front of the garage had been gravelled. Brenda had liked being able to say she had a gravelled drive until she found the cats using it as a giant litter tray. Brick paving swiftly replaced the gravel and Brenda had no difficulty in believing a woman who would allow her animals to do their business in other people's gravel would have no hesitation in encouraging Kevin to turn the garden into something not dissimilar to a compost heap.

It took a while and a cup of tea, but she made her mind up what she must do. There were only two possibilities; either the pond and the resulting bog went, or Kevin did. She was still unhappy with the idea of divorce, but there could be a separation and Brenda thought she liked the idea. There was something clean about the word "separate". It brought to mind separating the good from the bad, the clean from the dirty, the moral from the immoral.

She had not spoken to him in so long she was

not sure how to tackle the subject. As she scrubbed her bog-encrusted footprints from the kitchen floor she pondered on the matter, and somewhere between attacking the grouting with a toothbrush and wiping the soles of her shoes with wire wool, Brenda came up with a plan.

When he returned home from work that evening Kevin was surprised to find a decent meal waiting for him. It was true Brenda had been feeding him, but it consisted mainly of ready meals which could be heated in the microwave and eaten directly from the container. She did not approve of the smell of curry or any foreign foods, so it had been a dreary succession of shepherd's pie, liver and bacon or chicken stew in rotation. Before him now were the heady delights of a salad; true it was tinned salmon, but Kevin liked tinned salmon and there were hard-boiled eggs and new potatoes to go with it. Helping himself to bread and a lavish knob of butter he wondered what it was all in aid of. He got even more suspicious when she told him there was white chocolate cheesecake for pudding, but he was not one to look a gift horse in the mouth, so he ate all the salad and most of the cheesecake.

Brenda allowed him to eat before she tackled the subject uppermost in her mind, congratulating herself on the matter of the cheesecake. It had never before crossed her mind that chocolate could come in any other colour than brown. She put no curb on Kevin's cheesecake consumption and thereby made a mistake.

Replete as he had not been in weeks, Kevin dragged his bulging belly from the table to the living room and flopped down on the oatmeal sofa.

He turned on the television, flicked the remote a couple of times, then sank down into a post-gluttony sleep and could not be roused. He lay snoring and occasionally farting, his belt undone and his feet in their repellent socks resting on the coffee table (white oak).

Brenda watched him for a while until one gaseous eruption more pungent than the others sent her to the washing-up and then upstairs. She was done with planning and offering him a chance to redeem himself. She took a suitcase from the wardrobe ready to pack his belongings tomorrow. Separation from Kevin and all that came with him was now a necessity.

Before she went to bed she researched gardeners who could clear the pond away and restore the garden to some semblance of decency. She sent a few emails, but had a dreadful feeling it was not going to be easy finding one at this season. It was already the 20th of the month and they were all probably very busy.

* * *

Clues that all was not as it should be came early to Brenda the next day. She normally stayed in bed until eight o'clock to give Kevin time to leave the house. It crossed her mind she had not heard all the usual sounds that heralded this event, no muttered curses or cries of frustration over socks, pants and ties. When she went to the bathroom she noticed the lack of his telltale signs of occupation — no towels, no splashes of pee and no dollops of shaving cream left in the sink.

She glanced out of the landing window and saw the car was still in the drive. Thinking he must still be passed out on the sofa, she went down stairs to wake him and send him on his way.

He was not there, but his clothes were, trousers, belt, shirt, tie and underpants, all neatly folded and placed on the coffee table. His shoes were underneath.

What instinct told her he was in the garden she never knew or understood, but she did know and she went to the back door. She could see him — he was lying in the pond, his naked buttocks mooning the sky, his arms stretched out in front and his head under the water. For some bizarre reason, he was still wearing his socks, his toes buried deep in the mud of the bog garden as if he had been trying to find purchase.

For a while Brenda could think of nothing sensible to do. There were, of course any number of options. She could run down the garden to see if he was all right, despite the obvious evidence of her eyes, but she had never enjoyed the sight of Kevin naked, not even when they were first married. Instinct told her she was not going to like it any more today.

She could break down and cry, but as long as the mess that had been Kevin remained outside the house needing to be tidied up she could see nothing to be gained by such a display.

In fact, removing the unpleasantness that had once been Kevin was all she could think of. She picked up her phone and dialled 999.

For Brenda, the hours which followed were some of the worst she had ever experienced.

Within minutes the house had been full of people, all of them leaving dirty footprints over all the floors. She begged again and again for shoes to be removed, but no-one took any notice of her.

It began with the two paramedics, who took one look at Kevin and insisted the police should be called. They came back into the kitchen, treading mud and moss into the tiles, and despite her repeated request they refused to move Kevin out of the water and put him in the ambulance.

When the police did arrive they proved to be equally unhelpful. More mud was walked into the house and Kevin was still left where he was in the pond until a doctor had been called to pronounce life was extinct. There was then another delay while further officers were called. Brenda quite approved of these ones, they wore all-enveloping white coveralls which included their feet. The WPC who was sitting with her explained they were gathering forensic evidence just in case.

"In case of what?" Brenda asked.

The young policewoman seemed reluctant to go into detail, but she did suggest that Kevin's death might not be natural.

"But he died in a pond," Brenda said. "What could be more natural than that?"

The WPC did not have an answer to that.

It was several hours later when Kevin was finally removed, and despite their efforts to conceal it from her, the policemen were still laughing. Every time they thought she was out of earshot there would come the sounds of unbridled mirth, and if a new one arrived, he was taken quietly to one side, and after a brief whispered conversation, he would give a snort of humour which he would try to suppress, but never quite managed.

To be fair to them, they had tried to hide it from her, but when they finally lifted Kevin up they found he had a huge erection which for some reason had not relaxed in death.

It stopped them zipping him into the body bag until it was held down, but even so, once he was safe inside, it returned to its position at attention and made a small hillock in the top of the bag. Later the coroner told his assistant he had never seen a corpse with a more content expression.

A plain clothes officer who was having trouble keeping a straight face asked Brenda a number of questions. Did Kevin have any strange beliefs? Would she mind telling him a little about their sex life and the sort of things Kevin enjoyed doing? Had she any reason to think he might have had another interest, possibly a friend who might have encouraged him to experiment?

Brenda told him that as far as she knew Kevin was Church of England and she had no intention of discussing matters of a delicate nature with the likes of him. She did however mention the stranger she thought she had seen in the garden late at night.

The policeman made a note of this, but there was no forensic or DNA evidence to support the presence of another person near him at his time of death. The inquest recorded a verdict of death by misadventure, it being the opinion of the court that Kevin had died when some autoerotic asphyxiation experiment involving water had gone badly wrong.

This might and should have been a source of

much embarrassment to Brenda, but by the time the local newspaper came to print the story it was pushed to a back page by the extraordinary rebirth of the Ladybourne. After nearly a hundred years of being no more than a ditch, the river was again full of water. Behind the fence of Brenda's garden there now ran a sparkling young stream, full of water and fertility and all the sort of plants Kevin had grown in his (now filled in) bog garden flourished along its banks.

It was, as local people explained to the national newspaper reporters and television crews who came to view it, just like magic, as if something had sparked life into the ground and something wonderful had happened. The council said it was all a result of the rain they had been having.

Brenda sold number 27 as soon as probate was granted. Someone told her there was a good chance there would soon be water rats in the Ladybourne and that was enough to have her on the phone to an estate agent the second she got home.

With the money and Kevin's life insurance she was able to buy a nice one bedroom flat in a new block of flats. She nearly pulled out of the deal when she learnt it had been built on a brownfield site, but the developer told her he would lay white carpets in the lounge and bedroom, and then she felt better about the whole thing.

# MAUD: A GARDEN TALE

*"Come into the garden. Maud*
*For the black bat, night, has flown"*
Alfred, Lord Tennyson

Maud's earliest memories were of playing with earth and her first toy was a trowel.

Her parents were gardeners and they'd planted a tree for her as soon as she could get her tongue around *Quercus robur*.

She'd watched her father as he'd sunk his spade deep into the brown soil; watched as he disturbed the things that lived there and watched as he trod heavily on the earth pushing the roots of Maud's tree firmly deep down.

She'd shut her eyes when her mother had dropped her baby teeth into the hole.

"I've been saving them" she explained, "A part of you to be a part of your tree."

Maud watched the things the spade had disturbed burrow after them and amended her ideas about the tooth fairy.

\* \* \*

It was a long time before Maud realised that she didn't see the world the same way as others did. At first she thought this was because she didn't see her parents as other children did.

They weren't whole.

They were there, but Maud rarely saw all of them, she saw backs or behinds with only half a face turned away from the plants and the soil.

It was easier to join them facing the earth than to try and make them look at her.

They worked and Maud watched.

She watched the things that lived in the earth.

In the beginning she could only see the slow ones. They reminded her of the brown slugs drowned each night in the beer traps. They came when things were being planted and where there was fresh compost.

She told her mother about them and she said they were worms, but Maud knew what a worm looked like.

As she grew older and more independent her parents paid more and more attention to their plants and less and less to Maud. As their interest in her waned, the harder Maud looked at the garden.

She noticed the things that lived inside the trees; when she mentioned these to her mother she said they were called dryads and showed her pictures in a book.

Maud looked at them very hard, but the thin girls with wavy arms and floaty dresses bore no resemblance to the things Maud saw come out of the bark.

She didn't bother to tell them about what lurked at the bottom of the pond and made the

*Nymphaea odorata* die.

Most of the things living in the garden took little interest in either Maud or her parents. Occasionally one of them would be killed by a spade or a slicing hoe. The others would gather around the remains, divide them up and slowly eat them. Slowly and systematically grazing like the brown slugs did in the lettuce patch before their alcohol-sodden demise in the beer traps.

Maud watched each wake and wondered why her parents were unaware of the cannibal last rites they caused. And how they could be oblivious to the struggle of life and death that went on under the green water of the pond?

She still woke up in the night, remembering the screams when her father had emptied it and scraped away the thick layer on the bottom.

There was one part of the garden spared her parents relentless attention. Down the far end was an area set aside for "wildlife". Maud wondered if they knew just how wild life really was down there.

Amongst the grass tussocks and the hazel saplings Latin no longer ruled. Adder's Tongue and Hogweed grew there with Black Merrick and Rosebay Willowherb. Lords and Ladies changed from bright green to bright red, and Jacob's Ladder and Scentless Mayweed won the fight for life.

And the things that ruled the undergrowth weren't like the ones complacent of slaughter by steel tools.

They were *quite* different.

Maud watched them as they hunted; watched as they ate and watched as they fornicated amongst the leaves and the stems and the fungi.

A visitor on seeing this small savage wilderness asked Maud if there were fairies at the bottom of her garden.

"I suppose you could call them that," Maud said and wondered what there could possibly be to laugh at.

Maud's parents liked their flowers in their garden; only sometimes they would allow her to pick a bunch for the house, but Maud never considered it a treat. There was always at least one slow thing that managed to make its way in on a leaf.

It would die in the accumulated dust on the mantelpiece and fester there until swept away with the decaying petals that fell on its corpse.

Sometimes they would come in with freshly dug vegetables and Maud would watch them drown in the sink and be swept away down the plug hole.

The other things never came into the house, not until the Christmas of the living tree.

Normally her parents brought one from the garden centre, one grown to be cut. It normally came with a number of slow things, but they soon died.

That year her father decided to dig up the small fir tree that had grown in the wild part of the garden and put it in a pot.

"A living tree," he announced, "We can grow it on and bring it in every year."

Maud's mother thought it was a wonderful idea.

Maud watched the other things that had come in with the tree and thought it might just be a very bad idea.

She wondered if they'd die like the slow ones

did, but they showed no signs of it.

In the days leading up to Christmas they hunted through the house and many small things were lost or broken. Fresh fruit went white with mildew overnight and root vegetables went soft.

Maud sat in her chair and watched. She'd learnt more about sex than a child needed to know from watching them in the garden, but when they found the mistletoe that festooned the door frame she learned a great deal more.

By Christmas Day they were bold and drunk and mad with mistletoe.

Death stalked first the living room and then the dining room; they hunted each other through the discarded wrapping paper, under the tree and over the lunch table.

Maud ate her turkey and watched the pursuit around the cutlery, the ambush by the cruet and the murder done under the fatuous smile of the Father Christmas custard jug.

She watched the victor's dance of triumph. Watched as it made its way between the wine glasses and listened to the sound of the gloating. She watched as it ascended the mountain of the Christmas pudding her mother had placed on the table to carol its victory.

And she watched as her mother poured the flaming brandy over it and she listened to it scream and scream and scream.

The others stopped their howling and they looked.

They just looked for a very long time and then they all disappeared down one table leg.

Maud didn't eat any of the pudding.

And later in the evening she didn't eat any turkey sandwiches either or any Christmas cake.

They were all in the tree, amongst the baubles and the tinsel, and they watched her mother and father sitting close together on the sofa, a seed catalogue open on their laps.

At first they seemed unsure of where to go; they swarmed up the side of the sofa and began first in her mother's mouth. Several of them died there as she spoke excitedly about the possibilities of *Taxus bacata*.

They tried to burrow up her nose and down into her ears, but whatever they were looking for wasn't there.

Maud wondered what they were searching for until one of them began an exploration of her mother's feet and disappeared up her trouser leg. It returned seconds later and called to the others.

Her father remarked on the sudden unexpected draught and looked about for a door ajar or a window pane trembling.

They all disappeared up her mother's leg in a single column and Maud held her breath.

She was still holding her breath when they all came back down.

In the time between then and Twelfth Night they stayed in the tree and never left it; they sat and watched Maud's mother and Maud watched them. They were still in the tree when it went back out into the garden to be grown on for the next year.

It died in the spring.

Maud's father didn't often speak to her and never face to face. He told her the news while he was turning compost.

There was going to be a lovely surprise. It was a lovely surprise to him and mummy and he was sure it would be a lovely surprise for her.

In September there was going to be a little brother or sister for Maud and he hoped she would be a very good girl and help look after the new arrival.

Maud promised that she would watch it very carefully.

# HUSH-A-BYE

*"Hush-a-bye baby on the tree top*
*When the wind blows, the cradle will rock"*
Traditional

Morning light came through the diamond panes of the windows and sent beams of fragmented light across the breakfast table.

Angela lifted her teacup to her lips, then set it down quickly because her hand was shaking so badly she was slopping tea all over the cloth.

She looked across at John sitting opposite to see if he had noticed. He hadn't. He sat behind the Telegraph as usual and apart from the occasional rustle of paper and a grunt of annoyance when he read the editorial, the only sign of life was a hand which appeared every now and then to find a slice of toast or a cup of tea.

He ate and drank silently; even toast seemed to dissolve in his mouth, something Angela found very ironic.

Finally, he lowered the paper and for the first time that day acknowledged her existence.

"You look tired," he remarked. "Didn't you sleep well?"

Her fingers clenched on the handle of her teacup. "You know I didn't."

He faked surprise. He was she noted, not for the first time, very good at it, and said "I thought those new pills had made a difference."

The pills had been her doctor's idea.

"I'm afraid I can't take them, they make me feel sick and leave me dopey."

Again an Oscar winning performance, this time with added incredulous eyebrows and a small frown. "Why?"

She thought he was also a genius at changing the subject and she snapped. "How should I know, I'm not a bloody doctor."

It was a tactical error. She was now in the wrong and he was going to claim the moral high ground.

"Really, Angela," he said in a tone of gentle reproof. "Is that the sort of language to use in this of all houses."

She mentally compared what he had called the Prime Minister under his breath only five minutes before to her own milder invective and threw caution to the wind.

"What the *bloody hell* do you expect when I've had no sleep for weeks and weeks."

He clicked his tongue in disapproval, another habit she had come to hate and he made a small impatient gesture, dismissing her outburst. "You've never slept well all the years we have been married."

There was some truth in this, but he was using it as a weapon.

"As I have explained to you over those years, it's

hard to sleep through the noise," she replied. "And it's got worse recently."

"Has it?"

"Yes, and you know it."

His eyes sparkled at this and his lips curved into a smile, the one with a hint of triumph, the one which always made her want to hit him.

"*I* don't hear anything," he said.

There was a tiny snap and the handle of her cup broke. They both looked at it; the sharp edge had cut her finger and a tiny bit of blood showed on the white saucer. It was enough to spark him into action.

He made a great play of folding the newspaper and tucking it under his arm.

"I must be going, I've an important meeting."

As he rose she put out her now bloody hand to stop him. He was impatient of her touch, making small protesting noises as the gore stained his soft white skin, but she curled her fingers around his wrist and held it tight.

"I'm begging you, John. I haven't slept in months. If you've ever had any true feelings for me, please show it now and go and see a doctor!"

He peeled back her fingers and carefully wiped his hand with his handkerchief.

"I've told you before, my dear, it's *you* who need to see the doctor."

She took a deep breath.

"Please!"

He laughed heartily at this. Odd to think there was a time when she had found his laugh attractive.

"You keep telling me I'm keeping you awake",

he said, still chortling away. "But as I've explained again and again, my snoring doesn't keep *me* awake."

Bile rose to sear the back of her throat.

"Please," she repeated.

"Don't make a fuss," he snapped, losing patience. "Lay down in the afternoons and take a little nap while I'm out."

"I haven't got time to..."

But he was gone; running away from the conversation as he always did and leaving her to deal with the pile of his correspondence and the endless ringing of the telephone.

* * *

The advert was amongst the junk mail she separated from all the genuine letters. It took her most of the morning to pay bills and reply to requests for meetings, or invitations to attend conferences and to give speeches. The pleas for guidance she put aside for him to deal with.

She liked to check that junk really was junk, because occasionally there would be the sort of letter that is written in green ink and she always enjoyed what they had to say about John.

But this one was different. The words "Snoring Stopped: Success Guaranteed" were not something anyone in her position could afford to ignore.

Perhaps the lack of an address or addressee on the envelope should have worried her, but after a moment's consideration she found she was more than prepared to overlook this little diversion from the norm.

She picked up the phone and dialled the number.

\* \* \*

Success had its price, of course but doesn't everything? The man at the end of the phone was very firm about this and told her just what the expenses would be, but he was also very reassuring about the results and after thinking it through, Angela had no trouble agreeing the cost.

\* \* \*

Like most solutions to most problems, this one was not immediate. For another three nights Angela lay awake, looking up at the ceiling, sleep deprived, aching with tiredness, but no longer in despair.

Beside her John slept, his reverberations echoing around the room, a thin trail of dribble soaking his pillow. He slept soundly as he always slept, through the cacophony of grunts, moans and snorts, oblivious to everything.

"Soon," she thought. "Very soon."

\* \* \*

He never stirred on the fourth night when she got up and padded downstairs. She waited until the old clock on the sideboard softly chimed two o'clock, then she went to the front door. Moments later there was a soft knock and she silently undid the latch and opened it. A single hand appeared from the dark outside and handed her a small pastel pink box.

She had thought it would be black.

There was a soft chuckle as if her thought was known to the invisible courier. She resisted the temptation to sneak a look — the man on the phone had strongly advised against it, so she shut the door and went back upstairs on silent feet.

The bedroom reverberated with the cacophony that was John in the Land of Nod.

Even when she put the small sidelight on he never paused or turned over, he just filled the room with the thunder of his breathing, enhanced occasionally by a snort. Angela looked down at him, his mouth was so wide open she could see his tongue quivering.

She looked down at the box, having second thoughts about what she was contemplating doing, but as the only alternative she could think of was smothering him, she steeled herself to the deed. After all, he was a big man and it was possible he'd notice before she had a chance to finish him off.

Sitting at her dressing table she opened the box and pulled back the tissue paper inside.

They were so much smaller than she had expected, so tiny she was going to have to use the eyebrow tweezers to gently remove them from the box.

She went back to John's sleeping form. He was laying on his back, which was why he made so much noise, but it was also very convenient.

Carefully she lifted the first one from its fragile bed and laid it on John's upper lip, just below one nostril. At first it didn't move, then it slipped inside, pushing nose hair aside like a hunter moving through elephant grass.

Once it had gone, she laid the second one under John's other nostril and watched as it too disappeared.

She waited for a reaction, but nothing happened. John never woke and the sound of him having a good night's sleep continued without let up.

Angela watched him for an hour; then she went into the bathroom and had a bit of a cry. She took three of her pills and went to lay beside him and attempted to sleep.

* * *

The noise didn't stop that night or the next night. On the third day, during a long and tedious meeting, John ran amok and clubbed three of his fellow bishops to death with a candlestick. He chased another down a corridor, trying to stab him with a butter knife.

Then, to everyone's secret relief, he stripped naked and jumped off Lambeth Bridge. His body washed up on the next tide.

Everyone agreed it was a great kindness that Angela had been spared the ordeal of a trial.

# SAY "CHEESE"

*"Poets have been mysteriously silent on the subject of cheese."*
G.K. Chesterton

It is not easy for an ample woman burdened by a yoke and two five gallon buckets full of milk to run across a cobbled yard, but Gedy did a fairly good job of it, her bosom bouncing like a fishing smack in a gale and her clogs clattering on the cobbles like a set of false teeth in a politician's mouth.

The sound made an interesting accompaniment to her grunts of frustration as the buckets swayed in time with her bosom. She ignored the comments of the herdsman who was encouraging the cows back out to the grass; she was saving her breath for what might be going on inside her dairy, and annihilating him could wait for later. Inevitably her progress meant the odd splash of still warm milk slopped over, much to the delight of the scrawny cats that haunted the yard and barns, but at the moment this was bottom of Gedy's list of priorities.

She banged in through the dairy door and set the buckets down with a crash and yet another splash. After her race across the yard, the coolness of the dairy was welcome. The Earl's first wife had fancied herself as a dairymaid and he had indulged her with this perfect idea of a dairy to play her games in, all cool white marble surfaces and tiled walls. Rumour had it a year's revenue had been spent on the blue and white tiles with their pictures of frolicking calves and lovers dallying under hayricks.

Gedy had a low opinion of the calves and an even lower one of the lovers. The tiles might be easy to clean and they kept her little realm cool, but they gave certain people certain ideas.

Some of those ideas were being given life over by the settling pans.

"What is going on?" she asked in clear carrying tones which made the milk in the buckets tremble.

The man who was pinning the little girl to the wall turned to meet her gaze, but he did not do it for long. He turned his face away until he could remove the look of chagrin and replace it with one of condescending superiority.

"Good morning, diarywoman," he said in a voice as soft as a fresh cow pat and oozing like ripe Brie. "I'll be very surprised if that milk hasn't turned the time it has taken you to get it here. What can possibly have delayed you so long in the milking parlour, I wonder?"

Suppressing a desire to shove his fat greasy face down into the brimming whiteness of a bucket, Gedy ignored the implication and said, "Your concerns for the milk are always welcome, Master Ponton. Was that what you were... *discussing* with my assistant?"

Involuntarily Ponton's eyes went back to the thin little creature who was adjusting her crumpled clothing and setting her cap straight.

"I was merely advising Liene to show a little of her hair," he replied. "Modesty is very becoming in a maiden of course, but..."

"Very becoming," Gedy replied. "But stray hair in the butter isn't."

"No, of course not," he agreed. "And just how much butter are you producing?"

"Enough," Gedy replied.

"And that would be...?" He took out the small notebook and pencil which had become very familiar to the estate staff since he took up residence.

He held an ambiguous place in the household; he was some relative of the Earl's first wife, but not a close one. He was housed, but not in the best apartments; fed, but not always at table with the Earl. He was supposed to make himself useful, but he spent most of his time looking for faults and any woman who would not or could not refuse his advances.

Unfortunately, he did not annoy the Earl quite as much as he annoyed the Earl's staff and occasionally his little notebook was the source of unwanted and unnecessary inquiry.

"So much that we will be making cheese this morning," Gedy said. "Perhaps you would like to measure the milk?"

She handed him a very large and very heavy jug. Being as indolent as he was predatory, Ponton had no intention of doing any such thing, so he sought an escape route. He saw one in the yard behind her.

"There are a dozen cats gorging themselves on half an ocean of milk out in the yard. It seems a *vast* quantity of milk has been wasted already today."

Gedy shrugged her shoulders.

"It was only a drop. And the cats need the food if they are going to keep the rats down."

She deliberately emphasised the word '*rats*' as she looked at him and saw with some satisfaction a muscle in his cheek quiver as he fought to control his temper.

"Pints and pints wasted..." he said and made a note in the little book.

"There was a great deal of milk this morning," Gedy continued as if he had not spoken. "However, if you are concerned, I will report the wastage to the steward. No doubt he will consult you."

Ponton and the steward were not on the best of terms; the notebook disappeared.

"I mustn't keep you from your work," he said. "I expect that milk is already on the turn from the delay."

His eyes lingered on Liene and unconsciously his tongue slide from his mouth and circled his lips. The sound of clog on stone floor took his gaze back to Gedy. He opened his mouth to say something more, but changed his mind and left.

*Yes*, she thought. *You can bugger off. My last girl left with a fat belly of your making and I doubt if she was a willing partner. You aren't touching this one.*

"He'll get you into trouble," Liene said in her soft, lilting voice. It was a pleasing sound, full of the promise of music or maybe birdsong, very different from its waiflike owner.

"He'll try," Gedy agreed. "But I'm the best dairywoman in the county and worth more to the estate than he is. Now, did he hurt you?"

The small, thin little creature left the safety of the wall shaking her head.

"He was trying to put his hand up my skirt and my cap nearly came off, but you arrived."

"How did you manage to hold him off?" Gedy asked.

Liene shrugged. "I'm stronger than I look."

*I really must get some more cream inside her*, Gedy thought, as she always did when she considered the bone-thin child. She had been stuffing rich milk, thick cream and good butter into the girl ever since she arrived, but it never seemed to make much difference. *Ah well, maybe she is the lucky one*, Gedy reflected, aware of the effects the same delicacies had on her own generous form.

"Enough of this," she said. "Let's make cheese."

And that is what they did, filling the wooden cheese trough with the morning milk, then heating the previous evening's before adding it to bring the whole to the right temperature. Gedy showed Liene how to check it was warm enough, then how to mix in the precious rennet to form the curds. When the time came to separate them from the whey and begin the process of salting them and packing them into the cheese moulds, the girl proved to be a quick learner and Gedy was well pleased with her. She went into the cool marble lined room where the cheese was stored and retrieved a bowl of the clotted cream they had made the day before.

"Eat," she told the child, handing her a spoon and watching in satisfaction as it vanished. Gedy shook her head, again despairing of ever putting flesh on those thin bones, although she was not quite as thin as when Gedy first found her drinking the saucers of milk left out by the kitchen maids.

Someone had told the lazy sluts if they left milk or cream on the doorstep all their work would be done for them by magic and they had believed every word. Gedy had had quite a time defending her wares from the hussies, until they had looked out one evening and seen a very large badger devouring a dish of stolen cream.

She had little or no idea where Liene had come from, but there was a never-ending supply of wanderers and beggars and paupers on the road in these unsettled times and her instinct had been to mother this waif. She had not regretted her generosity. Liene worked hard and learned quickly.

*I just have to keep her away from that shite Ponton.*

In the days which followed the sun shone and the meadows flourished and so did the milk yield. Gedy and Liene had trouble getting the butter to take in the heat and had to beg ice from the kitchen. Ponton immediately protested the expense and out came his little notebook, but the steward silenced him, because the women were producing enough butter for not only the household's daily needs and to salt down for winter, but also a surplus which could be sent to market.

Until this, Ponton's interest in the dairy had been mainly in its occupants, but now he was interested in every gallon of milk that went in and what came out, and his little notebook filled with figures. Gedy became a little bothered. He might not be the steward's favourite person, but he did have the Earl's ear and any hints he might drop there could rebound via the steward to her little domain.

She was sure of her value and her position, but she did not want interference. If she chose to make a gift of a little butter or a cheese to someone, that was her perk and her right. Ponton watched her struggle back from the milking parlour with the brimming buckets of milk and seemed to be able to calculate exactly how much cream, butter and cheese she would get from each yield. She did not tell him the cream content would change as the summer faded; that bit of information was for her and the steward to know, but she was aware he would spot any deviations.

By midsummer every possible pot and barrel was stuffed to the brim with salty butter, fresh cream was being sent to the kitchen every day and what was not being sent Liene heated over the fire to clot, carefully skimming the yellow crust from the top of the warmed milk. The results acquired quite a reputation in the local market and the steward was well pleased with the profit.

He was even more pleased with the size and weight of the pigs, who had become quite blasé about the amount of whey they were being fed.

Cheese began to take up more and more of Gedy and Liene's time. They made curd cheese to be eaten immediately, balls of semi-hard cheese which ripened in a few weeks and wheels of a slow maturing one which began to fill the shelves in the cool room in anticipation of the cold season to come.

Gedy had little doubt that Ponton had been in there and made a note of exactly how many, which was why the accident bothered her more than it might.

That morning there had been more milk than they had expected and the buckets were so heavy even Gedy, strong as she was, could not manage to pour it into the cheese trough unaided. As she and Liene struggled with an overflowing bucket her hand slipped and the edge of the metal bucket caught Liene's arm, ripping open a long gash. Blood poured from the wound into the trough, leaving a swirl of scarlet snaking over the pure white surface.

Liene, paralysed with the horror, could only stand and watch as more of her blood dripped in.

"Come away, you silly girl," Gedy cried. "You're making it worse."

Liene snatched her arm back, and Gedy wrapped a cheese cloth around it and held it tight to stop the bleeding.

"What are we going to do?" Liene asked.

What were they to do? Gedy knew she should discard every drop of the milk, but she also knew Ponton would have made a note of the day's yield. She was not afraid of him as such, but she liked her pretty dairy with all its luxurious appointments and although she could find work on a dozen estates, she wanted to stay here. Matters of economy were a subject close to her noble employer's heart and it was a weakness Ponton relied on.

Grabbing one of the long wooden spoons, she quickly stirred the milk until there was no trace of tell-tale scarlet.

"That's what we're going to do," she said firmly. "And this."

She cast the rennet in.

"It's not warm enough!" Liene protested, but apparently, it was, because the curds began to form almost immediately. The two women looked down at the white mass gleaming through the opaque liquid.

"Not a word," Gedy said. "Not a single word. You go and turn the cheeses in the cold room. I'll deal with this."

From the back of the dairy she pulled out the huge cheese press, the one she had until now regarded as merely decorative.

The resulting wheel of cheese was enormous, so big it had to go on a shelf by itself, which suited Gedy perfectly as it was the deep bottom shelf and in semi-darkness and she could hide it behind any number of innocent cheeses. The whey she poured down the drain. The pigs were now so fat they would not notice the lack and it would do them no harm to be on short rations for one day. They did a bit of squealing, but Gedy "accidentally" left the sty door open and by the time they had been rounded up, their complaints about the lack of dairy delights went unnoticed and unconsidered.

The huge cheese sat undiscovered and isolated in its resting place for the rest of the summer. Gedy had no idea what she was going to do with it, but if anyone demanded an audit, she could produce it and say it was not yet ready to eat. She had heard of a cheese made in a foreign city far away that was left to mature for years. If it was found, by Ponton for example, or the steward, she would say it was one like that and it would be a while before it was ready. In time it would be forgotten.

Several times Gedy wondered if Ponton did know about the cheese. She had hidden it on the bottom shelf because she knew he was indolent, and bending down, possibly kneeling on the cold stone floor, was not something likely to appeal to him. And she had left him enough cheeses in full view to satisfy his little notebook.

He never said anything and she thrust her worries to the back of her mind.

She might have pushed her worry aside, but she could not forget the cheese. She checked it often, making sure it was well back on its cave-like shelf so it remained unobserved. It had developed a hard, crusty rind which in the normal way she would have been delighted to see. Again and again she wondered if the blood had introduced any sort of veining and in the end she could not resist the temptation to find out. She took out her trier and bored out a sample.

The long round core which came out was not what she had been expecting. The cheese was firm, but creamy and showed no sign of crumbling, it was smooth and if anything, paler than the norm. She sniffed it; the aroma was pleasant with a hint of sharpness and the faintest trace of the forest, the rich plummy scent of leaf mould and fungi and nuts. Gedy did what she would always do when testing a cheese, she broke a fragment from the end of the core to taste. The morsel was halfway to her lips when she heard a slight sound behind her and saw Liene standing in the doorway.

The girl's eyes were huge, great brown pools in the thin sharp framework of her cheeks and forehead. They reminded Gedy of chestnuts newly broken from their green cocoon. In their depths was a message, one she was not quite able to read. Silently she returned the piece to the end of the trier and pushed the core back in.

The little girl continued to regard her for a second; then gave a small nod and returned to whatever she had been doing before.

As summer drew towards its close the milk yield did not diminish, but the fat content did. There was less cream, but the demand from the kitchen for it and for butter and for curds to make cheese cakes and maids-of-honour increased as guests began to fill the house for the traditional autumn hunting.

Days were filled with the sound of the guns. Gedy and Liene had to put up with a steady flow of bored ladies who came to inspect the *"dear little dairy"* and listen to numerous comments along the lines of how much the bored ladies envied the two of them being able to play there every day.

The cheese room began to empty as round after round went up to the house to grace the dining table or to be used in the kitchen. Ponton was a frequent nuisance, dividing his time between demands they produce more butter, while at the same time accusing them of wasting whey or keeping it from the pigs.

Gedy ignored him. At this time of year when the fat was in short supply she was collecting whey cream to make butter and what was going to the pigs was not as fattening as before, but as their time in the world was fast coming to an end, she did not feel they really needed it.

He had been interfering in another way as well; when she checked the cold room one morning Gedy found the great cheese was gone. She was no fool and did not waste a second in speculating where it had gone. There was only one person who would have taken it.

He was waiting for her in the dairy. He had Liene by one arm and his other hand was inside her blouse kneading her small breast.

"Get your hands off her!" Gedy snarled.

He laughed and pulled the blouse open exposing the pale skin beneath.

"I think not," he said. "She is now mine to play with and you will be obeying my orders from now on."

His hands moved again, ripping the blouse away completely. His hand went to a knife at his belt and Liene tried to run, but he caught her by her cap and a handful of hair.

"No you don't," he said and sliced through the string holding her skirt. As she tried the hold on to the garment, her cap came away and her hair poured out and down her back.

"Very nice," he gloated, "Just the size I like."

Gedy rushed to try and protect the naked girl. She was so thin and frail, her bones like a bird, her tiny breasts as white as curd — only her long shining hair seemed to have strength. It cascaded down her back in a mass of shiny tendrils, the same chestnut brown as her huge eyes.

"Another step and I will hurt her," Ponton said, putting the knife to the child's throat.

"You'll hurt her anyway," Gedy said, but she stopped her advance.

"True," he agreed with a smirk. "But how much will depend on you."

"What do you want?"

He smirked at her, allowing his knife tip to play over Liene's pale skin.

"You thought you were being so clever," he said. "I knew there was milk missing and I wondered what you'd done with it. At first I thought you were selling it to line your own pockets, but then I found that great big cheese and I knew what you had been doing."

"I've been doing nothing!" she protested.

He shook his head in disbelief.

"I don't believe you," he replied. "I've thought for some time that you've been stealing, but I couldn't see how you were doing it, but of course, you've been making those huge cheeses and selling them. An easy way to disguise and transport what you've taken."

"You are talking rubbish," she cried.

"And that is another thing," he continued "You've got ideas above your station and think you can talk to me... me... any way you like, but now it is time to take you down to where you belong, under my thumb.

"That cheese is very best thing to come out of this dairy and making more of it will be one of the many little favours you are going to be doing for me from now on.

"I had it placed on the buffet last night and it

looked most impressive," he said. "It pleased my cousin to cut it with much ceremony and all the guests sampled it and all of them expressed their admiration for it. I told them it was made at my orders to my recipe and I am now commanded by no less a person than The Duchess herself to have one made and delivered to her."

"Your recipe?" Gedy repeated.

"Mine," he replied. "The first of those little favours you are going to do for me."

Gedy's replying smile was grim.

"I can't make another," she said.

"Why not!"

"Because there was an accident. Liene cut herself and some blood got into the milk. I knew you would want to know what had happened if I threw it away, so I made the cheese."

As she said it, Gedy wondered if it had been the most sensible thing to have done. If she had told the steward it could all have been sorted out, but for some reason it had seemed the right thing to do at the time.

"So, it needs blood to be special?"

Gedy nodded and then realised her mistake.

He looked about, his eyes wicked with frustration and anger; they took in the milk waiting in the trough and Liene, naked and vulncrable beside him. Swiftly, far too quickly for Gedy, he hauled the girl over to the trough, slashed her wrist and thrust the bleeding limb deep into creamy white depths.

"How long until the cheese will be ready?" he asked.

Gedy was a sensible woman, skilled at her work

and proud of her control over her domain, but she had no experience of violence and no idea what to do. She stood frozen to the spot, unable to make her mouth work or her legs move.

"How long?" Ponton demanded again, still pressing Liene's arm deep into the milk which had now lost its pristine whiteness and was blushing pink.

"Months," she finally babbled. "It will take months. Please let her go."

"Months?" he repeated in disgust. "You have to do better than that."

He thrust Liene away from him and Gedy ran to her, trying to stop the flow of blood from her wrist. It looked as if Ponton had cut some major vessel.

"Is she dead?" he asked, not much concerned.

"No," Gedy replied working hard to bind the wound and wrap her apron around the limp white form.

"Good," he replied. "We may need to bleed her again and I've not had her yet."

He turned away, picked up one of the long wooden spoons and began to stir.

"You're going to make me so rich," he told the circling milk. "And famous. Who would have thought what came out a cow's tits could be so valuable?"

And that was when Liene tipped him headfirst into the trough. He clawed frantically at the high straight sides and his feet thrashed about. Gedy wondered if the knocking sound was his head beating against the bottom, but before she could decide it stopped and a great many pink bubbles rose to the surface, popping in the fresh morning air, then he emptied his bladder all over her nice clean floor.

She had been rather fond of the trough. Over the years she had made a great deal of excellent cheese in it and spent even more time scrubbing it to pristine whiteness. It would cost her a great deal to see it burnt and a new one delivered by the estate's carpenter, but she could never again quite feel the same about the old one.

"What a waste of good milk," Liene remarked.

She was standing up now and there was no sign of any wound on her arm. This did not surprise Gedy as much as her apparent unconcern for her unclothed condition. Naked seemed to be as natural to her as a stout corset and two petticoats was to Gedy. She had even discarded her clogs and stood barefoot on the stone floor. The brown tendrils of her hair seemed to be moving, curling and curving around her thin shoulders and down to the two small dark nipples which crowned her tiny breasts.

"Maybe the pigs..." Gedy began, her mind looking for an escape and taking the one it knew best, milk.

"Best not," Liene replied.

A questing lock of hair lifted from her shoulder and wound itself around her neck. Their eyes met, Gedy's widening with understanding, Liene's ageless.

"Would you have helped?" Gedy asked. "For a saucer of milk?"

For the first time ever she heard Liene laugh, the bird sounds of her voice filling the dairy and the yard beyond.

"No, not for just a saucer of milk," she said.

Gedy's eyes went back to the pair of feet sticking up out of the milk.

"What am I going to do about him?" she wondered.

"He need not trouble you," Liene replied.

Gedy became angry with her,

"That is easy enough for you to say," she said. "You'll be... gone or away or whatever, but how am I to explain all this to the Earl?"

Liene lifted a finger, listening for something, and Gedy nearly fainted at the thought of who might be coming and what they might find.

There was a sound of running feet, soft padding on the cobbles, then the dairy was full of people, every space packed with thin, waiflike creatures with huge brown eyes. Gedy looked about her as they filled the shelves, sat in the settling pans, clung to the window sills and perched on the rim of the trough, stirring the milk with curious fingers and giving Ponton an occasional prod.

As she looked she began to recognise faces or thought she did. Two or three of them looked very like the bored ladies, another like the Earl, the one in the settling pan bore a strong resemblance to the steward, and surely the small one under the table looked like the boy who scrubbed the kitchen floor, whose nasty dirty little fingers got into every pot and plate not covered. There was even a couple of dogs milling around, strange thin dogs who wore the Earl's collar, but looked very different to the overfed brutes who snapped at everyone.

It took a moment, but she got there.

"They ate the cheese!"

"They did," Liene agreed.

"Did you plan it?"

"Certainly not!"

"But you did know what would happen?"

Liene shrugged.

At her gesture the creatures plunged their faces into the milk trough and drank, leaving Ponton high and almost dry, then they hauled his body out and sucked every drop of milk from him. Another gesture and they removed themselves and him.

"You needn't worry," Liene said. "Anyone who might have had a question won't be interested in the answers now. You will soon have new people to make cheese and butter for."

A cunning, calculating look passed across her face and tendrils of hair ran towards her mouth.

"You know if you ever need help, you only have to leave cream out. Only not a saucer. A bowl or two is better," Liene continued.

"There's a girl in the village..."

"I know the one, she will be most suitable."

Liene leaned forward and kissed Gedy's cheek. For a moment there was the fragrance of the woods, of earth and of trees, then the dairy was empty.

Gedy looked around her for a while,

*It's going to take me weeks to get this place clean*, she thought.

# THE GIRL IN THE WATER

He had not been sure before, none of the signals he expected had been made, but this morning she had looked his way as she stuffed her long curls under her swimming cap and he knew.

There was no doubt — she looked right at him, seeing him through the gap in his curtains.

She hadn't smiled, but he knew why. This relationship was their little secret and she didn't want to share it with anyone else.

His eyes followed her as she left the block of flats and made her way across the road to the beach. He stayed hidden because he didn't want anyone to know he was keeping guard over her, but he had to make sure she was safe, protected from any possible danger.

She understood this — he could tell. She even looked his way again as she flung off the towel she had draped around her shoulders, not openly of course, not enough to alert anyone, but enough to show how much she appreciated his discretion and his care. He noted the little telltale gestures with deep satisfaction.

The warm familiar glow began in the pit of his

stomach and began to heat his loins, but his brow puckered with displeasure as she stood revealed on the sand in her tight-fitting wet suit. Each morning she displayed every curve of her body to the watching world and he didn't like it.

But it didn't matter, because it wasn't going to go on for much longer; when they were together she wouldn't need to do it anymore.

She wouldn't need to swim either because, of course she'd only used her daily dip as a ruse to gain his attention, but that would no longer be necessary. Her every move, every expression which ran across her face and every flick of her long curls told him she was his.

He watched as she ran into the surf and swam out towards the horizon, an horizon that was frequently invisible on this cold coast; where the line between grey sky and grey sea was often indistinguishable. All he could see of her now was her white cap as she rose to breast the waves, and his erection rose to meet each forward thrust of her body.

He turned away from the window and his hand strayed to his boxers. They played this game every morning and every day it excited him, but it was now time to stop playing. It was time she stopped teasing him with pretended indifference and moved on to the next stage.

It was time to put all his plans into action. His hand moved rhythmically. She was going to be so pleased.

* * *

He knew where she worked; he had become a friend of the Sea Life Centre so he could attend the talks she gave. He loved sitting in the darkness as she spoke about sea urchins and anemones and fish. The rest of the audience thought she was speaking to them, but he knew every word was meant for him — it was just another part of the game they played.

A couple of times he'd approached her after the talks, when they all gathered for coffee and biscuits. He had stood as close to her as possible, making sure she knew he was there. Once he'd touched her arm, running his finger up from her wrist to her elbow. She'd jumped away from him as if she'd had an electric shock and he knew she'd felt the connection. She'd looked at him, her great dark eyes boring into him, speaking of passion, passion for him and him alone.

At first he thought he would go to her flat and just knock on the door, but that seemed so dull and boring after the fun they had had playing their game. He wanted to surprise her, to delight her, and he knew just turning up wouldn't be enough. She would expect more from him than that.

He checked all her doors and windows, visiting at times when he knew she would be out or sleeping, but he never found any of them unsecured.

For a while he was surprised and angry, very angry. He knew she wanted him, but for some reason she was making it hard for him and he didn't understand why. It took him a while, but then he realised it was *all part of the game*, making him work for his prize. She was such an adorable little tease.

He kept checking, waiting for the day when she gave in. It was a while, but one day when she was giving a guided tour of the Aquarium and he was there, just to check on her, she left her backpack on the desk in the lecture hall and her keys were inside.

He'd had to laugh; she *really was* such a little tease. It had been the work of moments to slip out of the centre and across the street to the key cutting booth. When he got back she was searching the floor for them and he had pretended to find them in the waste paper basket.

He loved playing these little games with her, but two could tease, he waited three whole days before he made use of the key.

When he let himself in to her flat, he'd lingered in the tiny hallway, running his fingers along every surface. He yearned to find her bedroom and to smell the air where she slept, but he made himself go to the living room, delaying the pleasure.

The room confused and annoyed him. Every wall was a bank of aquariums. Every available space was given over to a wall of water, it was like being at the bottom of the sea. All around him there was a steady throb as oxygen was pumped in and bubbles rose and fell and broke on the surface of the water. Green weeds swayed in the current, anemones waved their tentacles and fish swam back and forth, while the blue light sent odd shadows across the ceiling and floor.

He became angry. Why did she need these creatures when she had him?

He didn't like it!

He didn't like it one little bit; he didn't like it at the Aquarium and he didn't like it here. She knew he didn't. What was she thinking? It would all have to go.

He flung himself into the bedroom to wait for her. This was not the way it was supposed to be.

He was still annoyed when she came home, despite the soothing influence her underwear drawer had had upon him. Silk and lace had run through his fingers like soft rain. And the rubber of her wet suit had excited him more than he thought it would, the smell and the feel. He decided she would be allowed to keep it.

When she walked into the living room he was waiting behind the door.

To his astonishment and disgust, she pretended she didn't know who he was and wasn't expecting him.

She even screamed.

This was too much, this was taking their game beyond pleasure and into something he had not been prepared for, but if that was the way she wanted to play, he was willing. He felt a surge of excitement; she was even more desirable than he had ever dreamed possible when she tried to fight him off.

She was strong, but he was stronger. He clawed at her clothes, a little confused by her continued resistance, but more than willing to indulge.

At least he was until she dragged her nails down his face, hurting him badly and drawing blood.

Why was she doing this?

He searched for an answer and suddenly he knew why — it was because of the fish and the water. Her home was too much like her work. How could she relax and respond to him when she was surrounded by all these reminders of her job?

Silly girl, it was such an easy problem to solve. He flung her to the ground and began pulling the tanks down. In an orgy of destruction, he tumbled tank after tank. Glass exploded across the room and sea water fountained over her where she knelt on the now sodden floor. She was engulfed in a tide of fish and plants and sea life.

Satisfied he had solved the problem, he turned back to her, grabbing at her now soaking curls and pulling her head back. As he did so her voice rang out so loudly it popped his ear drums.

**"*Father!*"**

\* \* \*

The news reports said there had been a small earthquake out in the channel which had caused an unprecedented and localised tsunami. A small block of flats on the front had been destroyed, but only two people were known to be missing. The man's body was washed up down the coast, but, there was no trace of the young woman.

"Ironic that her name was Thetis," the coroner remarked to his clerk as he adjourned the inquest. "Makes you wonder where she ended up."

"Yes, sir," the clerk agreed, although he missed the irony.

# SWANSONG

*"So doth the swan her downy cygnets save"*
Shakespeare, *Henry VI Part One*

According to Gribble's mother Granny was a leftover, a last reminder of the time before when they had not lived by the marsh, but in it.

Granny told stories of wooden walkways over the water, of reed thatched huts raised up on poles and of strange creatures who dwelt in the still places and rode on the marsh gasses which sometimes rose up from out of the blackest water.

She was also supposed to have webbed feet. Apparently in the time long ago all the marsh folk had webbed feet, but as she never took off her thick oiled socks, at least not when Gribble was there, he never had a chance to find out if this was true.

She also knew lots about the birds, fish and animals which lived in amongst the reeds and the twisting water channels, knowledge that was useful, but she also knew every fanciful tale and legend attached to them. It was she who told him swans sing a beautiful song in their final moments and from that time on Gribble had one ambition in life — to hear a swan's death song.

He demanded more information, but Granny was not forthcoming.

"You stay away from swans," she told him.

"Why?"

"First off, because they can beat you senseless," she replied, although she seemed a little regretful having to impart this knowledge. "And second 'cos they are royal birds and not for the mishandling and pleasure of the likes of you."

"What's royal about 'em?"

The old lady gave a crack of laughter.

"They belongs to the Queen, sonny, and she don't take kindly to them being interfered with."

Gribble did not care much for Granny. She smelt of the oil she used in her sock wool and she monopolised the warmth from the fire. The feeling was mutual; she would watch him with eyes as hard as bog oak and never warned him of the dangers of everyday objects until the last possible moment. He took much of what she said as the ramblings of a demented old woman and, to be fair, he was not far wrong. Her notions about swans belonging to a queen were obviously one of those occasions when her grip on the real world had given way to the world in her addled head. Gribble had heard all about the nobs – kings and queens and lords and ladies, rich folks who every now and then came to the marshes to hunt. He also knew about the vast amount of fish and eels which had to be sent to them each year to pay something his mother called "taxes", but Gribble knew no-one owned the birds. They were there for whoever could take them.

His mother, who was forever busy at some task

or another once asked Granny why she disliked him so much. Gribble listened from the shadows, curious to know what he had done.

"He's like the marsh," Granny said. "Sometimes you step out of your boat onto what looks like solid ground only to find it is nothing more than floating vegetation waiting to deceive you. He may look solid, but he's deceiving you."

Mother had poured scorn on the suggestion and went back to her endless round of work.

When the winter came, bringing with it the rain and the cold and the fog, Granny's old lungs gave up the struggle to keep going and she was laid to rest in the soggy ground. Gribble was glad to see the back of her, but her tale of the swan's death song remained with him.

The fenlands were full of birds of every kind; some lived there all year, while others were visitors returning each winter and leaving again in the spring. Gribble listened to the sounds of grey geese as they filled the night sky with their cries as they began their flight away to the north and he longed to hear the sound a dying swan would make.

He reasoned if swans could sing and geese could honk on a journey, other birds might also perform at the time of their passing. Swans were big birds and hard for child to tackle, so he decided to start his exploration with small birds.

He began with ducklings, but all this proved was that young birds died very quickly from even the tiniest wound and rarely made much sound, and any they did make was far from satisfactory. Gribble reasoned they needed time to learn how to sing.

There had been a bit of unpleasantness when the owners of the ducklings found out where they were going, but Gribble's mother eventually managed to convince all concerned, including herself, it was all the fault of a fox, but even so, there were some suspicious glances and muttered comments.

Deprived of ducklings and feeling a need for privacy, Gribble gravitated to the wild fowl in the marsh. Here among the meandering water ways and vast reed beds no-one owned the ducks and the coots, the moorhens and the geese, and he was free to carry on with his experiments.

Not that it was easy — the birds nested and roosted in places it was hard to reach and they were wary. A couple of times he got into difficulties and nearly drowned in soft, soggy places deep amongst the reeds where no-one could see him. As he got better at finding his way and staying very still, he found the birds he wanted, but nothing sang for him. Even the bittern failed to boom as life drained away. It took time and a large number of assorted birds, but eventually Gribble was forced to the conclusion that only swans sang.

He needed a swan, obviously nothing else would do, but they were beyond him, no matter how hard he tried. One nearly broke his arm when he got near. The resulting bruises and blood had his mother nagging for days.

This was unusual, because his mother and his neighbours had long ago ceased to be concerned by what Gribble was doing alone in the marshes; as long as he was nowhere near them, it was fine. However, his activities did not go entirely unobserved, there were others just as interested in wildfowl as he was. They might have had different motives, but in their ignorance, they never considered his reasons might not be the same as theirs.

Wildfowlers hunted ducks and geese through the marshes and reed beds, supplementing the hunting with eel traps. Gribble often encountered them with their nets, their punts and their near-aquatic dogs. In time, they allowed him to join them, showing him how to pole the long shallow punts through the water, how to set the spring-loaded traps and where to find young birds on the nest. They explained to him how some birds like heron and cormorants could be taken to be raised in big sheds.

This bit of information made Gribble very excited, as he had never thought of taking a young bird and raising it to adulthood. He could steal cygnets, wait until they were big enough and then he could take his time getting them to sing. He nearly had an erection at the thought, but swans got very nasty when you approached a nest, very nasty indeed. If he was going to risk another encounter, he needed to know it was going to work.

Perhaps he could practice with a heron. It sounded as if they were easy to raise.

"Bloody hard work," one of the fowlers told him when he made a carefully worded enquiry. "My pa had me doing it — *helping* do it when I was a nipper. You have to have water for them, but because you have to keep them in the shed, they crap in it and if you don't keep changing it they sicken and die. Then you have to feed the evil bastards. They'd have your eye out as soon as look at you and getting piles of offal down them is not my idea of fun I can tell you."

"But they eat fish and frogs." Gribble protested.

"They does when they is catching their own, but not when they're shed-raised. They eat what comes, entrails and the like."

"But why keep them?" Gribble asked, it having occurred to him that herons were not noted for their death song, nor as far as he was aware were cormorants.

"To eat of course," they said, amused at his ignorance.

Gribble felt a rush of excitement course through his body like a wave of fire, it was all he could do to stop the shaking he felt in every limb. Like all marsh folk he had eaten the odd duck and goose, but mainly they lived on fish. It had never crossed his mind you could eat other types of birds and it never crossed his mind to wonder why he and his kind only ate duck and geese. If what these men said was true and you could eat heron and cormorant, then you could eat swan. The thought of *eating* the swan once it had sung and was dead, filled his head — he could consume it, take it into himself and make it be a part of him. The desire was stronger than anything he had ever experienced before.

"Can... can you eat swan?" he asked, trying to sound nonchalant, but desperate for confirmation.

"Well, you can," the fowler replied. "But the likes of you and me ain't allowed. They is food for nobs and kings only. Besides, they don't taste that good."

"You've tried it?"

"I'm not saying I have, but I am saying I wouldn't bother doing it again if I had. Which I haven't." Then he added, "An' I don't much care for heron either."

"What about cranes?" Gribble asked, eager for clarification. "Or grebe. Or cormorants. Or bittern. Or..."

"Just you hold up, young fellow. None of them is what I would call tasty, but they is *all* nob food, like those herons I helped raise. If you get caught with one that's not on its way to some lord's kitchen, you'll find yourself in real trouble. Even bigger trouble if it's a swan, they are..." he paused seeking for an unfamiliar word, "... *reserved.*"

Gribble wasn't paying a great deal of attention. His mind was full of possibilities, but one illogical fact rose to the surface of his churning brain.

"If they taste bad, why do nobs want to eat them?"

"Well, I reckon it's because there ain't enough of them to go round," was the reply. "If swans and the like were as common as eels, they wouldn't bother. Remember that young lord we took out two year back?"

This was addressed to another fowler, a small man who never said much and appeared nearer to a beaver than a person. Like Granny he was rumoured to have webbed toes.

"A right pillock," Gribble's mentor continued when he'd had confirmation of his memory. "He wouldn't eat my wife's eel pie, which she had put up especially for him, he'd only ate some sort of blackberry jam which tasted of fish and a cheese which was so far gone it nigh on ran off the bread.

He said both were expensive and hard to get hold of. He preferred that muck to good eel pie an' I reckon it was only because it was hard to get hold of and no other reason. Turning down good eel pie... ha!"

Gribble had tasted the eel pie made by the man's wife and was both fascinated and shocked. He would never have told his mother, but it really was the best he had ever eaten. The peculiarities of the nobility had distracted him for a while, but nothing ever wholly took his mind off his main purpose. It seemed more than likely someone who knew what swan tasted like despite apparently never having eaten it, would have been in the presence of a dying one, so he asked the question.

"What do they sing?"

"Who?" the man demanded. "Nobs?"

"No, swans. When they die."

There was a moment of stunned silence; then understanding broke through the dam of incomprehension.

"That old story! There's no truth in it," he said. "You ever heard a swan sing when it was killed, Sankey?"

The beaver man gave the matter some thought.

"No."

"What about other birds?"

Again the matter was given much thought, then he offered.

"A crane can give you a nasty nip if you're a bit slow."

Gribble was both disappointed by their answers and a little worried. That night as he lay in his bed he wondered how they could have missed the song.

It took him a while, but ultimately, he realised they had not been listening and they had been far, far too quick about the business. The song needed time and the only way to give it was to make the dying slow.

A wonderful truth crept into Gribble's head; swans were undoubtedly not the only creatures that sang at their death. They might sound the prettiest, but there were sure to be other things which sang and any one of them might sound as good as a swan, they might even sound better. It was the time they took dying which made the difference. If he could make it last the right length of time, he would hear them sing as well.

And then he could eat them.

This thought bounded out before he had gathered the strings of speculation. Fiery excitement again raced through him and rushed to his groin; he thought he needed to pee, but it was not urine which wanted an exit.

He thrust his hands deep into the feather pillow under his head, kneading the plump softness to relieve the tension. One of the things he liked most about birds was the feel of thin bones under soft plumage. The stiffer wing feathers repelled him, but the downy breast where the heart beat made his fingers itch to plunge into the warm depths and find the pulse of life.

Other things were soft and other things had small hearts which beat. These possibilities also crashed in upon him, filling his head with thoughts of the vocalisations of other soft pliable things, the baaing of lambs, the yip of a puppy, the mewling of kittens and the squeals of piglets. All of them came with the promise of a final song.

And there was the sound of children playing... but it was too soon. Gribble writhed and twisted in his blankets, trying to escape the sensations the idea brought, but it was too seductive a thought to dismiss lightly. It had sent the collywobbles prancing and dancing in his stomach and made the corners of his mouth rise involuntarily, so he locked it away in the recesses of his mind, in a deep dark place where he knew he could find it... *he could eat them...*

* * *

All these new ideas had given impetus to Gribble's need for a swan. By now he knew the wildfowlers were not going to hunt for any, so he gradually severed his ties with them, but not before they had shown him how to build a punt, or rather how to repair an old punt they had come across abandoned in the reeds.

They were concerned for the owner; there were eel traps nearby that had not been emptied and the punt had been secured.

"Easy for a man to fall in and get entangled in weed," they told him.

A few prods with a punt pole failed to produce a body and the general feeling was he had long since become eel food. Gribble had been fairly indifferent to the man's fate, but he was delighted with the punt. It was not large and many months of sun and rain and water had alternately swelled and shrunk the timbers, but a little work meant he had the means to explore the reed beds on his own.

He took to spending days alone in the marshes, taking care to return with a basket of fish to appease his nagging mother. She began to tell her neighbours he was just like his old granny, a true marsh man, web-footed and happier amongst the reeds than on dry land.

During this time, far from prying eyes, Gribble discovered what heron tasted like. The bird had not sung, he had not really expected it would, but the pleasure of watching it die and then eating the still warm flesh had made up for the lack of song.

It was alone in amongst the floating vegetation the idea of the swan bag came to Gribble. A way he could hold the bird secure, but leave the head and the long neck free. With the legs and feet held firm, he could give all his attention to the parts of the bird which most interested him. Making the bag, working out how to strap it closed took much experiment and used up a lot of cloth and leather.

These things did not come cheap and his mother was not only not in a position to provide him with funds, she was also unwilling to hand over what little she had, so Gribble had to go to work. He dug out old abandoned eel traps, cleaned them up and repaired them and then went out fishing. His mother was delighted that he was finally engaged in honest work and he even found some of the neighbours gave him the time of day.

It took a long time for him to save enough money to buy what he needed and even longer to make the bag, but in the end he created what he needed, a tube into which a swan could be pulled, strapped tight to keep the wings and the legs from moving, but leaving the head and neck free.

The next step was to find and capture a swan. Once this had seemed an impossible task, but during his time alone in the marsh Gribble had grown bigger and stronger and become very familiar with the ways through the reed beds. He knew where a dozen swans slept at night, standing on one leg with their head tucked under their wing. Poling silently and with the use of a dark lantern he thought he could creep up on a sleeping bird and have it secure in the bag before it had time to be aware of what was happening.

His first attempt ended in failure. He had not anticipated how much strength a swan had in its neck or the hissing and the pecking. Getting it in the bag had been relatively easy; the bird was disorientated by the light, but once awake the head had swung round in attack and in the confusion and his eagerness, Gribble ended up breaking its neck. It died swiftly without uttering a note. He was so annoyed he didn't even bother to see what it tasted like, he sunk the body into the water and poled away in disgust.

Controlling the head was a problem. Gribble resolved it quite easily with a sock – blinded and bound the bird became very still. Poling away deeper into the marsh, with the swan lying in the bottom of the punt, he planned the day to come, savouring every anticipated action.

The place he had chosen was one of the rare dry places to be found in the marsh, a hump of land rising above the water level. Surrounded by reeds, it was a rounded dome of low soft vegetation, a lovely, lonely place deep in the marsh and far away from any of the usual fishing places. Gribble had explored every inch of it and found it had not always been so lonely; there were traces of a hut still to be found and the blackened ring of a hearth. Whoever had once lived there was a memory from long ago, but there may have been visitors since. He had found a comb near the edge of the islet. It was made of some pale creamy stuff that was hard like wood, but was not wood, nor was it bone. Someone had taken the trouble to carve it into the shape of a swan and set a tiny red stone in it for the eye. Gribble considered giving it to his mother, but it pleased him so much he decided to keep it instead.

Here in his special place, away from the gaze of others, he was at leisure to find the truth of Granny's story. He became so enthralled by his work he no longer bothered to go home, living and sleeping on his island. When the smell and the flies became too much even for him, he went and slept in the punt for a while. In time the islet became white with feathers and bone, but Gribble still hadn't heard a swan sing.

As the days grew shorter and the night sky became full of the sounds of geese flying south, Gribble had begun to despair of hearing the sound he wanted to hear. He had lost track of the number of swans he had used up in his quest. He was beginning to wonder if Granny had been spinning him a tale, telling him it was swans that sang instead of other things; it would be the sort of nasty trick the old woman would have played. The possibilities of other creatures were starting to fill his mind and from the deep hidden place in his head the sound of children's laughter came to him.

This thought, mixed with the image of the swan on the comb was occupying him when he heard a sound completely alien to the world around him. He had been alone so long it took a while for him to recognise it — from somewhere among the reeds there was the sound of song. He shook his head, thinking it might be some buzzing bug struck in his ear, but the sweet sound persisted. Then, over the top of the reeds a swan appeared, at least the head of a swan appeared, one so huge Gribble could only goggle at it in wonder. It was so white it dazzled the eye and on its high elegant, elevated head it wore a little golden crown.

As he watched, his heart thumping, it came nearer and nearer, and as it did so it grew larger and larger and the song got louder. Gribble felt a surge of overwhelming joy, and tears welled up in his eyes. Here was a swan, a wondrous and enormous swan that had come here to die and he was at last hearing the song he had waited all his life to hear. His throat ached with emotion, he wanted to rush down into the water to embrace the creature, to feast on its beauty and its song as he would later feast on its flesh.

From amongst the reeds the full form of the giant came into view and as it did Gribble no longer felt the exultation he had been feeling, he felt fear. The swan was the prow of a barge rowed by a couple of servants and seated in the bow, attended by a young lady whose voice had until this moment been raised in song, and several gentlemen in hunting green, was a middle-aged woman with a back as straight as a punt pole and a nose worthy of a marsh harrier. She was also wearing a golden crown like the one on the swan.

The rowers had their back to him, so they did not see him, but they saw the expressions on the attendants' faces and risked a glance over their shoulders. One caught a crab as a result and there was a snapped word of reproof from one of the gentlemen, but the lady with the crown did not move a muscle or betray by so much as the flicker of an eyelid what she thought of what she was seeing.

The barge came to a soft landing on the islet and the rowers jumped out to tie her up. As they did so they saw the feathers and the bones and Gribble, and turned to their mistress for instruction. Her attendants were shouting and pointing, but the lady herself was silent and raised one imperious hand which silenced her companions.

She rose from her seat and as she did so, Gribble saw her deep blue cloak was trimmed with swansdown and high on the shoulder was an embroidered crest with a swan upon it. Gold threads glittered in the sunshine.

Gribble, who had been paralysed by fear, now understood why none of the dying swans had sung for him. The story had been about this woman — a swan lady, brought to him by a swan and wearing feathers. It was she who would sing for him. He ran to kneel before her.

The two rowers came up on either side of him, but he didn't notice them, nor was he concerned about the huntsmen, who were collecting parts of birds he had discarded, wings, heads and feet. They threw a pile down between him and the lady. Gribble was appalled by this disrespectful act — he would have shown her his work, explaining what he had done to each one, the care and the trouble he had taken to make it sing.

Her eyes flicked from Gribble to the remains and then back to Gribble, a crease forming between her brows. There seemed to be a question in her eyes, as if she was asking him something or waiting for him to say or do something. For a moment he was puzzled, then realisation broke over him like a blaze of light — she was asking him to help her die. It was time to use all the skills he had learnt in the slow torture of the birds to release her blood and watch it flow, until she reached the point where she would sing for him.

Tears of joy and gratitude ran down his face as he rose to his feet and drew out his knife. He knew just where he would start, a long shallow slice down her neck, just enough to make the blood run, but not enough to make it gush. His head reeled with the possibilities a human shaped body could have for other cuts, longer ones, deeper ones. Where to go next?

He wept even more when the knife was knocked out of his hand and he was dragged away from the lady. He screamed and shouted and tried to explain why she had to die, but no-one listened to him. He was still babbling about his need for blood and song when they bound him hand and foot and flung him into his punt. He promised them they could listen to the song with him, but they gagged him so he couldn't tell them what they would be missing.

They poled the punt through the reeds away from the island, deeper and deeper into the marsh, and when they came to a place where the channel closed and there was no escape, they dropped him into the water and watched him sink.

Later, a swan glided over the place and it looked down in the water and into Gribble's open staring lifeless eyes; then it turned and drifted away.

# CUSTARD CREAMS AND ELEMENTALS

Lionel's announcement that he needed to *"find himself"*, preferably with Sonia from Accounts, and to be rid of Marjorie and all her *"weird shit"* had been done over the kitchen table half way through a lamb casserole, two veg and a Duke of York's tart which had taken all afternoon to cook.

Marjorie watched him shovel another forkful of tart into his mouth, noticed for the first time just how much hair grew out of his ears and wondered why she'd married him.

What was he hoping to find? After twenty years she'd yet to discover he had any depths worth plumbing. And now she came to think about it, she'd never liked the name "Lionel."

As for the *"weird shit"*, he'd known about that right from the start. The very first time he'd come to pick her up for a date and seen the crystals on the shelf by the front door, he'd picked up three and juggled with them. She really should have known better then.

Without a word she cleared away her plate and went and collected all the crystals from downstairs, before going upstairs to remove the rest and her other belongings from the master bedroom and moving into them the spare room.

Then she went back down and erased the protecting ward from the front door.

\* \* \*

They didn't meet again for forty-eight hours. He was hunting through the fridge for something to eat, a hunt Marjorie knew with satisfaction would be fruitless. When he turned around she saw an elemental sitting on his shoulder. It was one of the more revolting types and was a disagreeable shade of puce. Normally her crystals and wards kept the little buggers from getting in.

She wondered where he'd picked it up.

"I've been to see my solicitor," he announced. "I will be keeping the house."

As she watched the elemental pushed its finger up its nose, had a bit of a root around and then wiped whatever it found in Lionel's ear hair.

"Mm?" she said, unable to drag her eyes away.

"I'm keeping the house," he repeated. "Sonia has a fancy to live here."

She didn't answer him, but the next day she found her own solicitor, a newly qualified young woman with all the charm of a rabid Rottweiler. When Marjorie told her about Lionel keeping the house, she showed her canines and said "We'll see about that."

The next time she saw Lionel he had a second elemental on his other shoulder.

\* \* \*

As she was no longer cooking Marjorie had taken to having lunch out and dining alone in her room on custard creams, apples and the occasional Mars bar. It was while she was having lunch that she was approached by an unknown woman.

She was about the same age as Marjorie, but fighting a rear-guard action to convince the rest of humanity she wasn't. On each side of her face, beneath the over-plucked eyebrows, an elemental pulled her crow's feet tight, while another two lifted her saggy chin. They were doing her no favours and they knew it. All four grinned at Marjorie and put their tongues out. They were, she noticed, the same shade of puce as the ones currently living on Lionel.

So much was now explained.

"You must be Sonia," she said. "You're not getting the house without paying for it."

The conversation which followed had the elementals rocking with laughter, but they kept a wary eye on Marjorie. The full and frank exchange of views between the two women had three results. First, Sonia imported several more elementals into the house via Lionel. Second, Lionel got an ear infection and third, Marjorie found the piece of paper which proved she had paid the deposit on the house out of her own savings.

The Rottweiler couldn't contain her delight and as a result, after the decree absolute had gone through Marjorie was able to buy her own little house.

It was charming, very small and very old and surprisingly cheap. Under the Victorian slate roof there was a good-sized bedroom and a neat bathroom and downstairs there was a large kitchen/dining room full of light and a tiny, cosy parlour with an open fire. It sat four square in a garden full of interest and surrounded by an ancient hedge.

There were other houses around, but they were only visible as the odd chimney or bit of roof over the hedge.

Marjorie loved it.

She had only been in residence for two days and was still surrounded by boxes when there was a knock on the back door. On opening it she was confronted by a monster.

Marjorie's first impression was astonishment. The monster was just under middle height, had hair of an odd shade not unlike Manuka honey, or it would have done if Manuka honey had golden syrup highlights applied in regular lines with the aid of a set square.

Dragging her eyes away from the hair, she was startled by a pair of eyes so blue it could only have been achieved by contact lenses and a set of creamy yellow dentures worthy of a Nile crocodile. She wasn't sure which scared her most, the dentures or the hair.

"Hello," the monster said. "I'm your neighbour from over the hedge. I've brought you some welcome to your new house biscuits."

There was something unstoppable about "welcome to your new house biscuits" and before Marjorie could stop her, the monster was over the threshold and sitting at the kitchen table in expectation of coffee.

She was also dripping with elementals.

It was only then Marjorie remembered she hadn't set out one crystal or applied a single ward to either door.

"I'm Mabel Louch," the monster announced. "I live just over the hedge in the bungalow. We share drains."

"Do we?" Marjorie asked, distracted by biscuits and elementals.

"We do," Mabel replied, obviously feeling this meant sisterhood of a no mean order. "I'm so delighted you've bought the cottage and I hope you'll stay a long, long time. This poor little house seems to change hands so often I'm surprised they haven't installed a revolving door."

She laughed and even the elementals winced at the sound.

Marjorie felt no surprise as she put the kettle on.

"I can't think why," Mabel was saying. "It's not as if we aren't welcoming. I'm sure I've never been anything but friendly."

She treated Marjorie to another flash of the Nile crocodile dentition and chattered away about a depressingly long list of former residents.

Putting the biscuits on a plate and mentally noting they were shop bought despite being conveyed in a tin, Marjorie poured the coffee and took a chair as far away from Mabel as she could.

Mabel did a lot more talking, her dentures spraying crumbs and coffee all over the table, but Marjorie wasn't really listening. She was watching the elemental currently lounging in Mabel's hair parting. Its hand was doing unspeakable things to an unspeakable part of its anatomy and it was depositing the result amongst the golden syrup bits.

Others were helping themselves to crumbs from Mabel's mouth and a couple were trying to get into her bra. They became aware of Marjorie's gaze and turned to stare back.

They knew damn well she could see them and they grinned, showing teeth just as disturbing as Mabel's, but a deep ruby red. On the whole, Marjorie preferred theirs.

"Now," Mabel announced, putting down her cup with a click. "I must see what you have done to the place."

And without another word she was off, scampering into the parlour and then galloping up the stairs to poke her nose into the bedroom and all the while she was scattering elementals, except for the one in her hair which seemed to be stuck.

As getting into all the rooms had been the purpose of her visit, she didn't stay much longer, but did ominously promise to be popping in fairly often to make sure Marjorie didn't get lonely.

Watching her trot down the garden path and through a gap in the hedge, Marjorie uttered the only word she could think of which summed up her feelings.

"Shit!"

Then she set to work arranging crystals and setting wards on the front and back doors. This would stop more of the little horrors getting in, but she was left with the problem of the ones Mabel had left behind.

* * *

It took two weeks to track all of them down. They were very good at hiding and Marjorie had a lot of spoiled food, endless creaking and rattling behind the skirting boards, and she never did find where they hid her spare car keys, library ticket or reading glasses.

Once she cornered one she was faced with the problem of what to do with it. Killing it took a lot of work and skill, plus she was always reluctant to kill anything and taking it back to Mabel might mean she passed it along to someone else.

She opted for her grandmother's solution – she bottled them. Each one had its own bottle, carefully corked, and she made sure to drop a custard cream in about once a week so they didn't starve.

Storing them was more of a problem. She certainly didn't want them in the kitchen, so she put the bottles out in the garden shed.

\* \* \*

Avoiding Mabel became a problem. What she called "popping in to see if she could be of any help" could happen twice a day if Marjorie wasn't very careful to lock doors, hide in the bathroom or go out.

Unfortunately, if she couldn't find her prey, Mabel would busy herself with "helping". This involved cutting back a climbing rose so hard it would be a couple of years before Marjorie had roses blooming over the front door, hoeing out a row of newly sprouted lettuce seedlings, removing the newly installed bolt on the gate in the hedge ("such a bother, dear, it stopped me coming to see you") and scattering slug pellets over the whole garden. It took Marjorie over a week to find them all and even then she thought she'd missed a few.

Keeping the shed door firmly locked was vital.

And it would have stayed shut if one of the local entrepreneurs hadn't decided to see if there was anything inside which would aid him in the pursuit of his business, this being making money from stuff he "found" and never doing a stroke of work.

At the time Marjorie was spending a couple of days with an elderly aunt and didn't discover the removal of her lawn mower and the breaking of her shed door until she returned, but Mabel had.

The police had been called, reports had been made, statements had been taken and utter indifference had been successfully concealed, but Mabel had unrestricted access to the shed.

Marjorie had barely got her key in the front door before Mabel "popped in" to see how she was and where she had been and who she had seen and what they had talked about. The "welcome home" cake bore a striking resemble to one frequently advertised on television.

"I've been very busy on your behalf, dear," Mabel announced, spreading cake crumbs and coffee drips much to the delight of her passengers. Marjorie noticed a couple of them had developed some sores which they were very proud of and improved by picking. What they did with the bits would have put her right off her slice of cake, but she was distracted by the gut clutching news that Mabel had been "helping" her.

The story of the break-in was told, but it was

what had followed that made Marjorie draw in her breath.

"Did you know there were lots of empty bottles in your shed? Well, I say empty, but someone had put old bits of biscuit in all of them, Very strange.

"It took me hours and two bottles of bleach to get them all clean. I flushed everything down your outside drain as I knew you wouldn't want that sort of thing in your sink. And, of course, you didn't leave me your spare key did you, dear. You really must, there might be an emergency."

Elementals and bleach.

The words kept revolving in Marjorie's head. Her grandmother had said something about it, but she couldn't quite remember what. She finally got rid of Mabel, but the question of elementals and bleach kept nagging at her.

The answer came about midnight when the drain from her cottage that ran under the hedge and on into Mabel's garden exploded. Unfortunately, or maybe fortunately, it exploded under Mabel's bungalow.

The engineers who came out to investigate the matter after Mabel's body had been removed and the remaining structure made safe, said they had no idea what had caused the accident and put it down to a freak of nature.

Marjorie thought the answer was elementary.

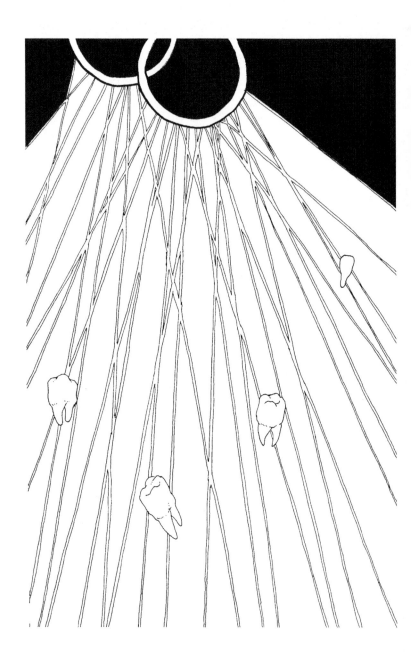

# NO SURE FOUNDATION

*"There is no sure foundation set on blood,*
*No certain life achieved by others' death"*
Shakespeare, *King John*

Of all the things Sylvia had planned for Tuesday, being dead wasn't one of them.

She'd got up at her usual time, half an hour before Terry so she'd time to wash and dress before him, and be downstairs to make him breakfast and pack his lunch. After he left for work she had a second coffee, and looked out onto her garden to make sure no inappropriate weed had sprung up overnight and check the cat from over the way wasn't doing its business in the flower bed.

Her eye was caught by a flash of hot pink and her nostrils flared; the tart from next door was standing on her patio smoking. Sylvia craned her neck and got sight of a pair of trousers so tight it looked like legs and backside had been whitewashed and a pink top so loose it was falling off one shoulder; it was obvious no bra was performing a fettering function.

Sylvia rearranged her own bosom to make sure

it didn't get any wayward ideas and drew back so Thea couldn't see her. When she and Terry had moved into Princes' Avenue, she'd gone next door to make the acquaintance of her new neighbour, but the sight of last night's dishes still in the sink at eleven o'clock in the morning, multiple coffee rings on the counter top and a cobweb of some size and antiquity hanging from the lampshade in the hall told her as much as she needed to know about Thea. This judgement was confirmed as her hostess was clad in little more than a silk dressing gown.

She'd told Terry all this and he'd said "Well, she's got the figure for it," and she was so cross she gave him egg and chips for tea two days running.

Sylvia sat back down at the kitchen table, spread out The Financial Times and smiled contentedly. This was her favourite time of day; Terry had buggered off down the M3 and she was alone to check her investments. She was pretty sure Terry had some suspicions regarding the state of her finances, but he was woefully ignorant of their extent and Sylvia had no intention of enlightening his ignorance. It had all started when she had been made redundant. She'd worked for the company for nearly twenty years, ever since she had left school, and they had been generous, very generous. The money, added to the nest egg she had inherited from an aunt, a sum Terry was also ignorant of, was enough to be exciting.

Given the chance Terry would have blown the lot on two weeks in Thailand and a new Audi, but he wasn't given the chance. Sylvia had instead discovered she had a gift for playing the markets;

she wasn't greedy and she wasn't reckless, and while there had been one or two bad buys, mainly she had by degrees doubled her savings and had every intention of doubling them again.

The FT was looking very pink in the morning sunshine, in fact it looked almost red. For a moment Sylvia was astonished at its rosy hue. It was as if a tide of crimson was spread out before her.

Then her face hit oil futures.

What followed was a period of darkness and confusion. When her sight cleared Sylvia took in the scene before her and knew she must be dreaming. It wasn't the sight of her body grotesquely slumped on the kitchen table, nor the mess of blood and brains which was soaking the paper, it was Terry. He was standing in the kitchen doorway when, by rights, he should have been halfway to work. Not only that, he was stark naked and holding a baseball bat.

Seeing Terry naked was to Sylvia like seeing a light bulb without a shade; in her eyes there were some things darkness and lampshades had been invented for. She opened her mouth to say something, but no sound came out. She tried waving her hands in front of his face, but he didn't seem to notice. When she looked at him he was wide-eyed, white and trembling. The baseball bat was caked in blood and what was probably bone and matted hair, but he lifted it and gave what had been Sylvia's head one more whack.

It was about then it crossed Sylvia's mind she might be dead. The need to consider this and to wonder about the lack of a tunnel with lights at the end meant she missed the next few minutes of the drama, but the sound of running water brought her back to what had once been her here and now,

Terry, still naked, was beginning to clean up!

In all the years they'd been married Sylvia had never known him so much as pick up a sock, but here he was pulling out buckets and sponges, mops and bottles of bleach. She found some comfort in the thought that her bashed-in head would make mess faster than he could clean, but he disappointed her by tying her head up in a pedal bin liner. He pulled her body off the table onto the floor and began to strip it, putting all the clothes straight into the washing machine and setting it on a boil wash.

The sight of a naked Terry washing her own naked body started a new sensation in Sylvia. Up until then she'd felt separate from what was before her, an almost clinical detachment, but really, this was going too far! Tiny flickers of rage began to sizzle.

She kicked Terry's raised buttocks and was aware that kicking Terry's backside had been something she'd wanted to do for years. By rights he should have felt something as her foot went through his rectal region, but he didn't so much as flinch. She tried again from the front; despite her foot going from his scrotum to under his chin and out through the bald spot on the top of his head he didn't pause in his sponging of her corpse.

Sylvia's sizzle surged from lightly browned to burnt black when the back door opened and Thea stood on the threshold. Terry might not have flinched at Sylvia's attack, but he jumped about three feet in the air when the door opened.

"Call the police!" Sylvia shouted, at least that's what she meant to shout, but no sound came from inside the pedal bin liner.

Thea looked from the body to the baseball bat under the tap and for a moment her eyes seemed to bulge in horror, but then her mouth opened and she ran her tongue around her coral painted lips.

"You did it," she said.

He let out a sound between a sob and a laugh.

"Just like we planned," he replied.

"*Just like we planned?*" Sylvia screamed. "*Just like we planned!*"

At least, that was what she tried to scream.

"Is everything ready?" Terry asked.

"Yes, I lifted the turf on the old air raid shelter last night. The hole is just big enough to drop her through."

Terry emptied a bucket of bloody water and went towards her his arms outstretched, but she backed away from him. He got the hurt puppy look he got when Sylvia gave him egg and chips two night's running or asked him to mow the lawn.

"We do it just the way we planned", he said. "In six months I'll report her missing, then when she never turns up I can have her declared dead."

"In seven years!" Thea pouted.

"But that will be seven years of interest on the savings, and I can sell the shares and this house and we can have our little bar in Spain."

"Are you sure?"

"Yes," he said, "We carry on as if she's alive. You come in and clean, and we have the groceries delivered like normal. She's not gone out much since she was made redundant. You go to the library once a month and use her ticket and I carry on doing all her on-line banking..."

"*How did you find my password!?*"

"... no-one will guess she's not alive."

"What about...?" Thea gestured to the body.

"I'm going to clean everywhere, make sure there's not a trace of her in here or on me. Winter is nearly here and down in the shelter with the turf relaid she shouldn't cause problems — no smell. Or at least not much and there are plenty of things which will... um... tidy her away. I'll wait until its dark and bring her over."

Thea slipped away and Sylvia watched as Terry built up more of a sweat than he had in years. She considered his cleaning; practise makes perfect and Terry had never had any practise. She noticed he'd missed a small splash of blood, which had seeped into the hinge of one of the kitchen cupboards, and the tiny bone fragment, which had lodged under the fridge. Would he, she wondered, be stupid enough to remove her rings? He was rolling her onto a sheet of plastic when he noticed them and she watched with cynical amusement his internal debate. It was odd how detached she was now from everything except a slow burning rage.

Terry removed the broad gold band and the nice solitaire which had been her mother's. He was still undecided, then he had a light bulb moment and, folding them into a piece of kitchen roll, he went and put them at the back of the old pantry, pushing them deep into a crack in the plaster Sylvia had asked him to fill every week for the last five years.

Her rage flared again; she loved that cupboard

with its deep marble shelves and the jars and jars of jams and preserves she made. One thing was for sure, when Terry had eaten all the pickled onions he was never going to taste one better than hers ever again.

In the hours following Terry showered twice and gave another clean to everything he could think of. He washed Sylvia's clothes a second time before throwing them into the tumble dryer. Her fake fur slippers gave him trouble; they looked like a pair of cow pats when he finally got all the blood out of them, so reluctantly he chopped them into tiny pieces and buried them in the compost heap.

When darkness came he waited until well past midnight to move Sylvia's body. She was delighted to find rigor mortis had set in and she was about as easy to move as a plank. It took him an hour of sweating and heaving and biting back swear words to get her over the fence and into Thea's garden.

Sylvia felt an irresistible urge to go after. She was totally disgusted to find she had to follow her remains down into the dark hole in the middle of next door's lawn. She landed in the bottom of a black pit smelling of damp and ancient vegetation; it was a fair drop and she landed with an audible thump, which made Terry nearly pee himself. He lay flat on the grass and used his phone to illuminate the hole, and Sylvia got a good look at what was left of the old air raid shelter. It was only a moment before Terry pulled a board over the opening and rolled back the turf.

And that was it.

Sylvia sat in the darkness beside her body and brooded. She worked out she was probably a ghost, but never having been dead before and never having had any sort of psychic experience she was making assumptions with very little evidence; for all she knew everyone who died ended up hanging around like a fart in a lift. Deeper and more profound thought suggested this delay in whatever was supposed to happen next might have something to do with how she'd got to this point.

Sometime around dawn there were developments. Firstly Sylvia took objection to the colour her skin was going, secondly a solitary fly managed to find its way through a tiny gap in between the turf and the edge of the board — Sylvia could almost hear it say "yummy!" — and thirdly she felt a need to do more to Terry than just kick his testicles. In fact, she really, really wanted him to suffer.

This thought stopped her being bored for several days, plus the fly had been joined by others and what was happening, while in its own way fascinating, didn't do much for Sylvia's sense of self-worth. She thought she was going to be stuck down there forever, or until someone noticed the smell and phoned the council, until she noticed a thin line of something, she had no idea what, which went from her, up onto the lawn, over the fence and into her house. It was not difficult to follow it and when she walked through the kitchen door — and she did walk *through* it — she saw it branched into three strings, one to the cupboard hinge, one to the bone fragment and one, much stronger, to where her rings were hidden.

*Hello, Terry*, Sylvia thought and smiled.

She might have smiled, but over the next few months being able to access the kitchen didn't give her much satisfaction. She did find another fragile thread to the living room where enough skin cells had accumulated in the upholstery to give her a tether, and the thread to the bedroom and bathroom had been stronger until Terry bleached her toothbrush, scrubbed her hairbrush and comb, and either washed all her clothes or had them dry-cleaned. Now only her jewellery box held traces of her.

It galled her, but Terry was being far cleverer than she'd ever given him credit for. He made sure all the things she paid for were paid out of her bank account, he did on-line shopping as she had, even though it all went over the fence to next door. He visited her Facebook page, played the odd game and scattered a few "likes". She'd never had much of a social life outside of work and being made redundant had cut her off from that world; people always say they will keep in touch, but very few do and the couple of calls Terry got were easily put off by saying she was out.

The only constant in her life had been the library, two crime fiction and two romances every four weeks. She thought someone might notice it wasn't her using the ticket, but no-one did, and it was Thea who went and maintained her presence. And no-one noticed Terry nipping over the fence every night after he'd turned all the downstairs lights out and gone through a pantomime of turning on and off the bedroom and bathroom lights.

Sylvia yearned to make him aware of her, to scare the ungrateful, adulterous lard bucket out of his wits, but she'd no means of reaching him. He'd eliminated every trace of her physical being from his life and while her fingers longed to claw his eyes out, there was nothing to hang on to.

Time went on and to all intents and purposes, she went on in the real world, just as she went on in the existence she now had. She wasn't bored as such, but she sometimes had a feeling of being pulled somewhere else, which she ignored. In the end, of course, Terry got bored with coming home each evening to no dinner and a continuous regime of cleaning in order to maintain the appearance of Sylvia being alive and well, and armed with a mop and broom. Sylvia didn't know for certain, but she was fairly sure whatever sustenance awaited him after his nocturnal fence climbing was not a patch on what he was used to. She'd seen the rise in biscuits and pork pies in the weekly delivery.

Her suspicions were confirmed when a very sulky looking Thea let herself in at the back door and spent the next hour running a none-too-clean duster over a limited selection of surfaces. She looked in at the bathroom, but apart from pouring half a bottle of bleach down the loo she didn't do much more. She dragged the vacuum cleaner into the main bedroom, but apart from plugging it in she did nothing more because the wardrobe and the chest of drawers acted on her like a magnet. She flicked garments along the rails in the wardrobe, but none seemed to please her very much and she shut it without taking anything out.

The chest of drawers was of more interest. She pulled out a cashmere sweater which had miraculously escaped Terry's favourite boil wash. She held it up against herself, but eventually rejected it. A rummage produced several packs of unopened tights which she put in a pocket. Sylvia tried putting her hands around her throat, but there was no reaction.

On the other hand, when Thea opened the jewellery box on the top of the chest Sylvia felt her anchoring thread grow a little stronger. A long pink enamelled nail stirred the baubles and she lifted out the small sapphire pendant which had been Terry's wedding present. It glittered in the light, and she was starting to fasten it around her neck when Sylvia found there was a trace of herself on the ornament and it was drawing her closer and closer to Thea. She put out an experimental hand and sunk it deep into the younger woman's chest.

Thea gave a gasp, clutched at her bosom and spun round.

"Who's there?" she demanded, the note of panic delighting and surprising Sylvia.

She was so surprised she had no time to take advantage of the situation; Thea flung the necklace back in the box and was halfway down the stairs and out of the back door faster than a pizza delivery driver on a deadline.

*How interesting,* Sylvia thought. *How very interesting.*

She awaited developments with eager anticipation and felt deep satisfaction when Terry didn't stay with Thea that night. He returned home after midnight with his mouth the shape of a cat's behind. He stamped upstairs, flung himself into his neglected bed, taking time only to punch the life out of the innocent pillows.

He stayed away from Thea for nearly a week, but then he was once again fence-vaulting in the middle of the night. Thea returned as well, waving a reluctant duster about and pushing the vacuum cleaner at any uncluttered space, but only downstairs. She never ventured upstairs again.

Sylvia's remains had been in the air raid shelter for six months and no-one had noticed, at least no-one with only two legs; those with multiple legs knew all about her One day in late April Terry took a day off work and spent a hour selecting a full set of Sylvia's clothes, including shoes; he carefully packed them into several neat brown paper parcels. He was gone a couple of hours and when he came back he didn't have any parcels. A week later he made a phone call to the local police station and reported Sylvia missing; he gave them a careful description of her and a detailed account of what she'd been wearing when he last saw her. He listened carefully to the officer explaining when adults go missing there is often an innocent reason, so no action could be taken straight away. He expressed deep concern about this delay.

"But it's not like her," he wailed with Oscar winning conviction and an expression of smug satisfaction. Sylvia tried to smack him around the head, but to no purpose.

An officer did come to see him, took in the pristine state of the house and the well-stocked cupboards,and enquired about anything missing. Terry told him about some clothes he couldn't account for and the deeply sympathetic policeman explained again it wasn't uncommon for ladies of a certain age to leave their home and family for no apparent reason. He hinted at hormones, but he promised they would look into things just in case.

"Try not to worry too much, sir. I wouldn't be

surprised if she turned up in a week or two."

The officer put a hand on Terry's heaving shoulder and never saw the smile buried in a handkerchief.

For the next month or so Terry had no trouble maintaining his role as the concerned husband. He made a total nuisance of himself with the police and only just "allowed" himself to be talked out of putting an advert in the local paper offering a substantial reward for information on Sylvia's whereabouts. He enjoyed himself enormously, added beer to his weekly shopping delivery and toasted Sylvia's absence most evenings.

Sylvia wanted to shove the bottle either down his throat or upwards through another opening. She was so angry she didn't at first notice the lack of Thea. Terry still spent time next door, but it seemed to Sylvia it wasn't as frequent as before. In time she also noticed a diminishing of Terry's euphoria. She wondered if it was guilt, but she found that hard to believe.

He did a lot of drinking and even more sighing, and his underpants seemed to be too small for him. Sylvia finally put two and two together and came up with a double D cup and a bottom too big for the jeans covering it.

All was not well with the lovers and Sylvia couldn't have been more delighted.

After a solid fortnight of unrequited lust Terry was as relaxed as a hedgehog in the fast lane. He brooded and gnawed his lip and did things in the bathroom Sylvia had no trouble in not watching. She wondered if he might go to the police and confess out of sheer frustration, but he came up with a plan. Sylvia knew he'd had a light bulb moment because he began to dig around in the airing cupboard to find the good table linen. He spent a whole evening reading cookery books. He got more and more morose as he worked his way from Delia to Nigella via Mary, and Sylvia was not surprised when he came home with three carrier bags of luxury ready meals.

He read all the cooking instructions twice, before setting the kitchen table with care and candles; then he opened two bottles of red wine and Sylvia nearly died a second time when she saw the label. He went into the deep larder and after a bit of excavating with kebab skewer he dug out the two rings he'd hidden months before. Sylvia closed her fingers around his throat and squeezed until her hands passed right through, but he didn't react. The wedding band got a bit of a polish; he considered it for a moment; then returned it to its plaster nest, but the diamond solitaire was held up to the light and it flashed fire around the room.

Sylvia felt the cellular pull of whatever bits of her were still embedded in the mounting. She tried to remove one of Terry's eyeballs with her finger while he gloated over the diamond, but to no avail; her fingers just slipped unfelt through to his brain. She wasn't surprised — he always did have the sensitivity of a tapeworm — but she'd a very good idea what he had planned for her ring and the recipient, while indifferent to the social norms regarding sex with your murdered neighbour's husband, did have the capacity to feel Sylvia's presence. Sylvia was looking forward to scaring the knickers off the bitch when she slipped that ring on to her finger.

At first Thea was a reluctant diner, but as the scallops and prawns disappeared and the first bottle of wine had taken a bashing — Sylvia noted only Terry would have served red wine with shellfish — she began to relax. Beef bourguignon, seasonal vegetables and the rest of the bottle and most of the next made her very mellow indeed. She was positively glowing after panna cotta and the last of the wine.

Smirking like a teenager who has discovered his father's porn stash, Terry put coffee, a plate of chocolate truffles and glasses of brandy on the table and Thea beamed at him with alcohol-fuelled affection. There followed a lot of face sucking and truffle sharing. Sylvia did her best to join in, running her fingers through Thea's hair and running her hand down her spine, but either the lack of contact with something Sylvia-based or alcoholic intervention meant she failed to get a response.

Terry was equally wine-fuelled, but had something on his mind, so after removing his tongue from Thea's mouth he embarked on a slurry declaration of eternal love; then he took Thea's left hand and slipped the solitaire onto her ring finger.

At first there was no reaction or response from Thea, so Sylvia decided to help things along by giving her wrist a Chinese burn worthy of the best playground bully. There was a brief moment of total stillness: Terry still held Thea's hand and still beamed like cartoon moon high on weed, but then Thea went rigid and sober in the time it took for Terry to say "I love you."

What followed was the best entertainment Sylvia had ever had; it made being dead almost worthwhile.

Thea did a lot of screaming and when she found the ring was stuck on she did a lot of threshing about. Terry made the mistake of trying to help and she stopped trying to get the ring off so she could hit him. It was all set to the sound of Thea screaming "No! No! It's hers, she'll get me!" and "She'll find me!" and "Get it off! Get it off!," while Terry harmonised along the lines of "Hold still, you stupid bitch!" and "Don't talk rubbish!"

Eventually Terry was winded by the edge of the table being shoved into his groin. He went backwards, landing heavily and painfully in his overturned chair. Thea, finally managing to haul the ring from her finger, flung it at his head and fled through the back door, her moaning wails being heard by half a dozen interested neighbours.

Sylvia was delighted. It had all gone so very well.

It took Terry a while to get his breath back. When he did, he found his body needed to get rid of a very expensive meal and some very expensive wine very quickly. He was left weak and shaking, and more than a little annoyed. He kept muttering "Stupid bitch!" to himself as he scrabbled around on the floor looking for the discarded ring. He finally found it and made his way to the larder, intending to put the ring back in its hidey-hole, but once inside he felt shaky again. He stumbled and hit his head on one of the marble shelves. This alone might just have stunned him, but a large jar of Sylvia's best pickle onions fell on his head and cracked his skull.

It took the SOCOs a while to work out what had happened. By the time Thea decided to check on him he had been dead for two days, and it was another two weeks before her nerve broke and she rang the police. By then vinegar and an assortment of lively maggots had been at work.

It had taken a while for him to die. Sylvia had sat beside him and waited, fascinated by the slow exit he made, so unlike her own departure. Alive Terry had been unaware of her presence and untouched by her attempts to harm him, so he was at first astonished find her looking at him. She allowed him a few seconds to join the pieces together; his own unmoving carcass and the set of green, dripping bones standing over him. All those multi-legged beasties had enjoyed themselves enormously in the air raid shelter under the lawn.

He screamed, or at least his ghost screamed and tried to run, but being a ghost takes practise and Sylvia was nearly a year ahead of him. She stretched out one skeletal finger and wriggled it around in his eyeball; it did feel nice and best of all, he had another one.

She was quite disappointed when the forensic team found and removed the fragment of her tooth and the trace of blood. The link which held her to the house and access to Terry were gone, and she was confined to the shelter. It was all very boring, but when people in white protective jumpsuits lifted the grass and began to remove what they found there, she became very tired and slowly drifted into a darker place.

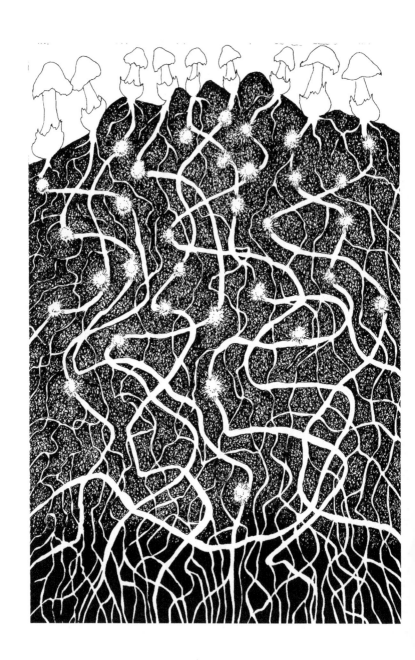

# A SOLEMN CURFEW

*"... to make midnight mushrooms, that rejoice to hear*
*the solemn curfew."*
Shakespeare, *The Tempest*

The heat in the kitchen, which had been intense
earlier, had now reached the point where the sweat
was not only running down Quine's face and neck,
but also down his back to gather in the crease of his
buttocks and begin to drip from between his legs,
pooling on the floor at his feet. He flicked his head
to one side to dislodge the bead of moisture from
the end of his nose and stop it falling into the dish
he was preparing for his Lordship's table.

Like every other man in the kitchen he was
working naked but for clogs and the large bib
apron which protected him from the assaults of the
ovens, spits and braziers. The heat of the open fires
worked its way into every part of the men, scarring
their flesh with sudden splashes of boiling fat or
sugar and, unknown to any of them, grilling their
testicles and putting paid to any hopes of
fatherhood.

Quine had been in the kitchen since dawn, long

before all the other cooks, except for the bakers heating their ovens for the dozens and dozens of loaves the great household needed every day. He came early not to cook the vegetable side dishes that would grace his lord's table, but to prepare what was needed by the other cooks as part of their offerings. In these early hours he and his scullions would finely chop and slice piles of celery, carrots and onions, mince oozing bowls of crushed garlic and reduce mounds of assorted herbs to a fine green dust to enhance and scatter over meat, fish and pies.

He hated this work, hated wasting his knife skills on the offerings of others. He wanted to devote his time to the dishes he sent for approval at the high table of Castle Gregannor.

He looked up from the asparagus he was preparing to snarl at the two young scullions who should be shelling a bushel of peas, but who were instead giggling and wriggling their bottoms in the direction of the head chef sitting enthroned in the middle of the bustling inferno. He was supposed to be supervising every station of his domain — meat, fish, breads, sauces, vegetables and the intricacies of the dessert, pies, pastries and confectionery, but he was easily distracted by a pert behind as every boy in the kitchen knew.

Quine growled at them and they turned again to their work, occasionally exchanging glances and poorly suppressed laughter. They knew he had very little authority over them and an appeal to the head chef would undoubtedly lead to the remittance of any punishment. They knew he would not allow their main assets to be disfigured with stripes.

The peas were finally freed from their pods and Quine began preparations for cooking them. He visualised a perfect green hillock in a pure white bowl, he would allow them just the right amount of time in boiling water flavoured with a little mint and enough sugar to enhance their sweetness without turning them into a sickly mess, then he would dress them with butter and cream and more mint, carefully and artistically scattered over the top.

As he cast the peas into the water, the head chef's voice cut across the kitchen.

"Quine! As soon as they're cooked, you can give them to Dorton to garnish the ducks."

Quine stiffened with rage. This happened again and again — his vegetables, his hard work, his skills were taken away from him to adorn the work of others. At least once a week his lordship would send his compliments to the kitchen on some dish which had delighted him. With his compliments would come a coin, sometimes a silver one, or a glass of wine.

There had been times when Quine had been allowed to taste the wine; occasionally the lucky cook would share his reward with those who had helped him create the masterpiece. Even now, angry as he was, he could remember the bouquet of the wine and its colour like liquid sunshine. And it had tasted of sunshine, the rich glow of the sun in autumn just before the leaves begin to turn and the harvest is ripe and abundant.

The memory of it clung to his tongue like a lover's kiss and he yearned to taste it again — almost as much as he yearned to slip a silver coin into his pocket, many, many silver coins. The trouble was, he never got any recognition for the dishes he sent to table, they were merely a chorus to the main players the other stations sent up.

A dish of perfectly steamed marrow, no matter how skilfully it was dressed with minced egg yolks and scarlet pepper, could not compete with a peacock roasted and presented wearing its tail feathers or a whole turbot nearly as big as a table.

And far too often he never even got to send dishes up. What he had prepared was taken away to be the garnish or decoration to some other offering. He wept when he remembered the precious truffles which had gone to his lordship speared on skewers with some cockscombs just to decorate a venison pasty. What he could have done with them!

The peas went to Dorton, and Quine began preparing batons of salsify dipped in breadcrumbs and deep fried. He wondered if he could speak to the steward and get him to bring the dish to the attention of the top table. Normally nothing left the kitchen without the approval of the head chef. Everything was presented to him on his throne and he would inspect it, sometimes tasting a part, before it was handed to the steward who saw it on its way to the dining hall.

Quine knew if he showed up the salsify it was very possible it would never leave the kitchen. It would be deemed too unsophisticated, too rustic, and it would be added to a grander offering. The one thing it would not be was discarded. Quine allowed himself a cynical smile; it might not be visually spectacular, but it was delicious, far too delicious to waste. If it did not go to his lord's table, it would certainly make its way into the head chef's abundant paunch.

Greatly daring, Quine decided to defy him and accost the steward directly. The salsify batons came out of the hot fat and he saw they were golden brown and crisp. He quickly dusted them with best sea salt and then carried them to where the harassed little man was directing the waiting men and the scuttling pages.

"A delicacy for my lord." Quine told him.

"Very good," the steward said, gesturing to a boy to take the plate.

Quine watched it go, turned a triumphant smirk on the now fuming head chef and returned to his asparagus. He was certain such a treat could not fail to please and he was probably right, it might have done if it had reached its intended diner, but Quine had made a mistake of cutting his batons into convenient inch long pieces and by the time every page had helped himself to just one bit, the plate that reached the hall was so denuded it was not considered worthy of his lordship's table. It was sent to one below the salt, where it was very much enjoyed by those without the palate to know just how lucky they were.

The gambit had failed and it had also put the head chef's back up. Quine found he was not allowed to send a single dish to the hall; everything he prepared and cooked was taken to be part of another's creation. His anger and humiliation knew no bounds, but although he might rage to himself and weep tears of frustrated fury into his early morning preparation, no means of revenge presented itself, nor did any means of bringing his skills to the attention of the noble family he served.

* * *

The steward was a man who knew little peace or tranquillity. The place he occupied between the kitchen and the hall was not an enviable one. He was responsible for seeing only the best of what left the kitchen went before his lord, but he also had to make sure honoured guests were fed according to their rank and to ensure none of the lesser folk below the salt went hungry or accidentally got anything intended for their betters.

If this alone was not enough to worry the man to a peptic ulcer and a nervous tic, he also had to make sure the waiters, the carvers and the pages knew their work and their place. Supervising the correct and elegant portioning of dishes and keeping potentially grubby fingers out of them, as well as making sure it all arrived in front of the correct recipient called for vigilance and cunning.

However, he was not an unkind man, and always having one eye on the kitchen he was fully aware of Quine's dilemma. He sympathised with him because within the confines of his chosen section, Quine was a genius. The head chef and many of the noble dinners might not notice the humbler offerings which graced their meals, but the steward who got to eat a lot of them knew they were often missing a culinary treat. He decided to give Quine what help he could.

Most of the vegetables for the kitchens came from Castle Gregannor's own gardens. Each morning the head gardener or one of his men would appear with trugs full of what was in season or what they had forced into growth. It was a matter of some pride to the outside staff that they could furnish the kitchens with all the fruit, vegetables, herbs and flowers they could want or need.

The head chef was always polite to them because he needed what they grew, but he was nowhere near as effusive in his gratitude as he was to the gamekeepers and the stockmen, or even to the egg woman and the girls from the dairy who brought cream, butter and cheese.

This had not passed unnoticed, and at the behest of the steward, the gardeners began to bring the more unusual and exotic vegetables, things they grew for their own interest and pleasure, direct to Quine.

Unfortunately, the head chef scuppered this ploy with ruthless efficiency. The colourful striped beans went around a dish of stewed larks, the purple stalks of chard added excitement to a boiled ham and the odd little knobbly white tubers baked in lard never made it out of the kitchen, another casualty of the head chef's appetite for the exquisitely delicious.

None of this escaped the steward, so he tried a change of tactic. His lordship, he informed the domestic tyrant, was extremely fond of all forms of mushroom and had expressed surprise at how rarely he saw them at his table.

The chef protested, pointing out the number of black truffles which appeared as decoration and the delicate shavings of white truffle that he himself added to omelettes and other eggy offerings. The steward acknowledged this, but said variety was required and he was going to arrange the supply.

After this estate workers and, more frequently, their children, began appearing at the back door with baskets full of things they had foraged from the fields and hedgerows.

Much of what they brought was not fungi and Quine rejected it as unfit for a noble table, keeping only the wild garlic, the sorrel and some of the other leaves to add piquancy to some dishes, but what delighted him most were the various mushrooms that arrived and he began to experiment in his very limited time.

He was no fool; he knew the dangers which came with them. Identification was vital, literally the difference between life and death, so he took advice from an old hag in the village who delighted in trying to get him to taste unknown examples. At first he had done so, assuming she would not allow him to eat anything which would kill him, but after one night spent in agony crouched over the latrine hole he knew he was wrong.

When confronted, she had just laughed and told him he would not make that mistake again. And he did not, only agreeing to try one if she did so first. Not everything was worth the effort; some types did not taste of anything very much, others exuded a rather disgusting looking liquid which tasted fine, but looked vile, but in the end he had a selection he knew was safe and either tasted wonderful or were beautiful enough to make up for their lack of flavour.

He started slowly, not wanting to create a sensation before he had established a reputation for his fungi. The first thing he sent was a simple stew of field mushrooms seasoned with a hint of thyme, a little nutmeg and a lot of butter. The head chef eyed it and Quine saw the flash of greed in his eyes. For a second he thought it was going to be rejected and then consumed by the bastard, but a loud clearing of throat sound came from the steward standing in the doorway and reluctantly the dish disappeared out of the room and made its way up, down the corridors to where light and music flowed from the great hall.

There was no wine or coin, but there was a small nod from the steward and Quine thought he would burst with pride. He went to bed dreaming of a time when he would have enough money saved to tell the head chef to shove a globe artichoke up his rear, and go out into the world to start his own restaurant.

This small but exclusive establishment had been imagined and designed and yearned over for a long, long time. It would serve meat and fish and poultry, but these would only be there to complement the vegetable dishes Quine would invent to go with them. He would build a discerning clientele who would understand that a perfectly poached beetroot was as much a pleasure as any hunk of bloody steak or roasted fowl.

In the days which followed Quine was able to send a fungi dish to table at least once a week, sometimes more. There were very thin slices of grilled puffball rolled and filled with a mousse of wild sorrel, penny buns in a cream sauce, and golden chanterelles on pieces of fried bread. All of these got the same nod from the steward, but none brought the longed for reward.

What did bring it was an amusing dish of amethyst deceivers and scarlet hood. It was not the greatest tasting dish in the world, but the colours were exceptionally pleasing. It was not my lord who sent the glass of wine, but my lady, who had been enchanted by the combination.

Now Quine became more daring, sending a dish with chicken-of-the-woods. He was taking a chance with this, because they could make some people unwell. Unfortunately, there was no way of knowing who this would be until they had eaten it. They had had no effect on Quine and had been so toothsome that he had decided to risk it.

Fortunately they had no effect on his lordship either, but they did on the scullion who had sneaked a taste while Quine's back was turned and the head chef who had done the same. On this occasion, Quine had no regrets about the lack of recognition, his reward was the sound of his enemy puking his guts up. It was days before he was able to look at the head chef without smirking.

His moment of triumph came when he sent up a dish of white onion risotto topped with black horns of plenty. He was cooking celery in cream when the noise in the kitchen suddenly died away and he looked up to see a page come in carrying a goblet.

All eyes followed the boy's progress and they grew wide with astonishment when he went straight to Quine and inclined his head.

"With my lord's compliments," he said and

handed the goblet over.

The wine tasted just as it had before, only better. He took his time over the glorious golden liquid, savouring every precious drop and every envious look sent his way. He carefully returned the goblet to the page; it was made of glass and probably worth more than his year's wages.

It was a while before the silence in the kitchen was broken and work resumed.

The morels gave Quine his ultimate moment. A child of a particularly revolting uncleanliness presented itself at the door of the kitchen. There was no way of discerning its sex, it was so filthy, ragged, rank and repellent. Its grubby hands gripped a bag brimming over with fresh morels.

Quine immediately set his scullions to the task of cleaning them, carefully dipping them in freshly drawn water and then drying them on new linen. Still not happy he gave each a goose feather and told them to clean every nook and cranny.

They grumbled of course, so to their utter astonishment he applied the flat of his palette knife to their unprotected buttocks. He saw the head chef start up to protest, so he did it again to show all three of them who was in charge of the section. There were no more protests from any of the parties concerned, and although both the boys sulked, the morels were cleaned to Quine's satisfaction.

There were so many of this precious fungus Quine felt able to give some to the poultry cook to garnish a boned and rolled chicken. The glow of pleasure he got from being able to make this gesture was almost as great as the one he had got from disciplining his disrespectful staff.

He then set about producing a mixed vegetable mousse set in aspic and decorated with not only the morels, but also with tiny diamonds of thinly sliced carrot, shreds of green bean, discs of radish and diced black olives. The result was breathtaking, a translucent flower garden planted with trees.

When it was borne away from the kitchen, there were reluctant nods of approval from all his colleagues, bar one. The head chef watched him with cold dangerous eyes, but Quine did not care.

He cared even less when a page came back and handed him not a silver coin, but a gold one. It was a very small, but it was gold. If the head chef's eyes had been cold before, now they blazed with suppressed fury.

\* \* \*

It took less than a week for the shine to come off Quine's surface. In the battle of the servings and the heady moments of triumph he had overlooked an unpalatable truth, for the seasons of the year were turning and the time of the mushroom harvest was fast ending.

Although he had spent many hours at the end of each service drying any number of fungi in the cooling bread ovens, Quine knew he would have trouble stretching out this store until the next time treasures started to appear under the trees and hedges. It was soon apparent to him that another person had realised his period of culinary stardom was about to come to an end. The head chef, silent and brooding for the last few weeks, began a quick return to the old ways of doing things.

Carefully julienned leeks went off to adorn some fish, artichoke hearts which had taken hours to prepare were taken and ruthlessly sliced into a rabbit stew and a pile of ruby chard had been sent up under a swan.

Quine also made a complete mess of a pumpkin. Every cook has a bad day and every cook has one thing they never quite manage to cook properly, and for Quine it was members of the squash family. He usually delegated them to his staff, but the head chef was as aware of his weakness and ordered them again and again, and demanded the head of vegetables prepare them himself.

Open defiance would have been a serious mistake; as much as Quine wanted to leave Castle Gregannor and go his own way, his savings made this an impossible dream. He might not like his job and he might loathe the head chef, but both of them were preferable to tramping the open road looking for work. So he bit his lip and did his best with the hated ingredient, occasionally raiding his stock of dried fungi to create a dish worth sending.

One evening, after the fourth attempt to season a spiced butternut squash soup to the standard expected of a nobleman's kitchen, Quine took the risk of approaching the steward again.

He was shaking his head over the soup and directing one of the waiters to serve it to the lower orders when Quine finally caught his eye.

"You are letting me down, my friend," the steward said. "I went to a great deal of trouble over you."

"I know," Quine replied. "But what can I do? Is there some other side dish which would please his lordship?"

"None I can think of. He is not a man to be pleased with greens."

"Onions perhaps?" Quine said, desperately.

The steward pulled a face.

"My lady can be very unpleasant on the subject of bad breath, but I will admit my lord is fond of such things."

With this information, Quine returned to his section and produced a huge mound of fried battered onion rings. He made enough to allow for the inevitable losses on the way to table, but still leave an abundance to be presented to his lordship.

When a young woman dressed in my lady's colours appeared in the kitchen Quine thought for a second he had triumphed again, until she spoke.

"I have a message for you, cook, from my mistress. If you dare send such a dish as those onions to her husband again, she will see to it your mouth is washed out with horse shit. Then you will know how she feels when she has to sleep with a man whose breath smells like the wind that blows from Satan's arse."

With this she smiled sweetly and left. Behind Quine the rest of the kitchen staff gave way to laughter.

* * *

In the days which followed Quine became more and more desperate. All the hard earned respect he had won disappeared and his scullions, now free from any fear of retribution, reverted to giggling idleness and flirting outrageously with the head chef.

He lay awake at night, exhausted by the long hours of work, but sleep always eluded him. He turned over idea after idea in his head, but as hard as he might worry away at the problem, his imagination could never hit on the thing which would make everything right again.

He needed a special dish, one which would shine like a beacon amongst all the others; something so flavourful and so delicious strong men would weep for joy when they put it in their mouths. As he listened to the reverberating snores of his fellow servants through the hangings which separated them and to the softer sounds of bare feet padding in the direction of the head chef's bed, he curled up into a ball and allowed the agony of self-pity to slice through him like his own paring knife.

As a section head he had the privilege of a bed to himself, but there was no advantage in it. He might not welcome the presence of a boy under his covers, but he often longed to feel the soft naked flesh of a woman. That was another possibility which had now disappeared; a few more weeks of good dishes would have seen any number of ambitious females only too eager to enjoy his success and all the things it might bring.

He could of course have paid for the comfort and several maids had offered to help him part with his savings, but his desire to leave Castle Gregannor was greater than his lust and he kept his purse as tight closed as his loincloth.

Quine might not have been able to see a way to change his predicament, but fate arrived in the form of a travelling spice seller. They went from noble house to noble house and from manor to manor and farm to farm, selling the expensive luxuries which could not be grown in the gardens or the fields. For those who could afford to buy they brought such things as nutmeg, cinnamon and cloves, as well as candied oranges, raisins, dates and sugar.

The first and most urgent need in the kitchen was for sugar. Quine paid very little attention as the head chef negotiated with the young man who had arrived with his wagon and mules; spices were useful, but he generally used what was in store and any herbs the man might have been carrying would be dried and he had his own source of them, so he was surprised when the head chef barked a demand for his attention.

"This man tells me he has green lentils. He seems to think you would be interested."

Quine was definitely interested. He had a good store of the yellow ones, but the superior and rarer green ones did not often come his way.

"Come out to the wagon, good sir," the merchant said. "You can see for yourself how fine they are."

Nothing loath, Quine made his way out to the courtyard where the wagon stood. It was a neat and well maintained conveyance and the two mules were strong and shining with health. This spoke well for the quality of the merchandise inside, as did the young man who was in charge of it all.

He could have been no more than thirty;

medium height and build with a bright, cheerful face, and he showed a set of good white teeth when he smiled.

"My name is Hurl," he said, thrusting a well-manicured hand towards Quine.

"Quine," the owner muttered, taking the hand.

"Come and see my excellent lentils."

The inside of the wagon smelt wonderfully of spices and sweetness and a deeper more subtle aroma like an exotic perfume. Hurl pushed aside small sacks and boxes, clearing a way to the back of the wagon where larger sacks and bigger boxes stood.

He pulled one of the sacks into the middle of the cleared space and untied the string holding it together. He plunged a hand inside and held out a fist full of dark grey-green lentils.

"The very best," he said, allowing them to spill back into the sack. Quine thrust his own hand into the sack and inspected the pulses he pulled out. Hurl was right; they were of the highest standard and he was already thinking about how he would cook them when something small, round and blue caught his eye.

All thought of lentils vanished from his head. They were mushrooms — there were only three of them, but they were obviously fresh.

"What are they?" he asked, trying to keep his voice calm.

Hurl followed his gaze and shrugged.

"I've no idea," he replied. "I found them growing where I camped a few nights ago. I didn't recognise the variety, but the colour is so unusual I thought I would cut a few and see if I could find someone who could tell me if they are good to eat or have some other use. I wouldn't want to miss the chance of a quick cash crop."

Trying very hard to stop his hands from shaking Quine picked up one of the mushrooms. It was the same shape as a penny bun, but smaller and a totally different colour. As he turned it towards the light the blue colour became more pronounced and when he turned it over the gills beneath were almost purple.

They smelt heavenly; they had been the source of the scent in the wagon, the aromas of the forest mixed with an earthy pungency and just a hint of something else, a herb maybe, possibly chervil.

"Were there many of them?" Quine asked. Even to his own ears his voice sounded squeaky.

"Quite a few," Hurl replied. "Do you know what sort they are? I would hate to poison someone."

"No," Quine answered. "But I know someone who might. I could take these to them if you like?"

He waited, holding his breath.

"Would you?" Hurl said, obviously delighted. "I would be very grateful."

He took Quine's hand again and shook it warmly.

"Here," he said. "Take them all, I've got some business at the next manor, but I will come back this way in a few days and maybe then you'll be able to tell me if I should go back and fill some baskets or put up a warning sign."

Quine dutifully laughed at this, but he was careful to conceal his discovery in his apron pocket when he returned to the kitchen with the lentils. He could barely control his excitement through the long day of service, but finally the last dish left the kitchen and he was able to order his two boys to clean up while he dressed. Keeping a weather eye on the activity going on around him, he stole a small white loaf from under the noses of the bakers and went out into the late afternoon sunshine.

Once he was clear of the castle walls he took out his new mushrooms and gloated over them. A cautious voice in his head warned him they might not be safe, but their heady aroma and strangely beautiful colour was so attractive he could not bring himself to believe they might be dangerous.

However, it did no harm to check and he went to the cottage of his old hag to see what she made of them. She was sitting by her fire stirring something in a pot which made Quine recoil in horror.

She saw his reaction and laughed.

"Hungry?" she asked.

"No," Quine replied without hesitation. "Here, eat this instead."

She snatched the bread away from him and broke a piece off, rapidly proving that a single brown tooth was enough to tackle new white bread.

"What do you want?" she asked. "You must want something or you wouldn't have bought this."

She took another bite of bread.

"Just some of your knowledge, mother," he replied and laid one of the mushrooms before her.

She frowned and picked it up, turning it over in her hands. She inspected it carefully and then smelt it.

"Smells all right," she said, handing it back.

"I know that," he replied, "What I want to know

is what sort it is and if it can be eaten."

She considered the fungus again, masticating thoughtfully as she did so.

"No idea," she said, shoving the last of the bread into her mouth.

"What do you mean, no idea?"

"What I said. I've never seen this sort before."

This was not what Quine had wanted to hear.

"Do you know if it's poisonous?"

"Not a clue. But I know a way to find out."

"How?" Quine asked eagerly.

"Eat it," she said and howled with laughter.

Quine made his way back to the kitchens livid with anger and half tempted to throw the blue mushrooms away, but their heady aroma came wafting up to his nose and he found his mouth was watering. An idea came, a dangerous idea, but one which might be worth a chance.

If these mushrooms were as delicious to eat as they smelt, a plateful of them would do more than just delight a mushroom lover, like his Lordship, it would enchant him. Add this to the nobility's love of the rare, the unusual and the expensive and he could be sure of goblets of golden wine and plenty of golden coins. He would also regain the position of envy and respect in the kitchen which had been his for those few brief months.

He decided he would eat one and see what happened.

Looking at the small treasure in his hand he was tempted to try it raw, but the hag had told him right from the very beginning that many mushrooms were toxic, but could be rendered harmless and edible by cooking. He decided he would cook one before eating it and he would do it first thing in the morning before anyone else was in the kitchen. If he was going to have a reaction he needed to be awake to see what it was and if he was going to die, and the idea did make him shudder a bit, he wanted to die in the kitchen where it would cause the most disruption and ruin the head chef's day.

He had a disturbed night full of anxious dreams which jerked him awake. It was during one of these wakeful periods he heard a whispered conversation between his two scullions; it resulted in the elder one making his way to the alcove where the head chef slept. Hours later in the first pale light of pre-dawn Quine heard the boy making his way back to the pallet he shared with his co-worker and knew he would be very likely be losing the better trained member of his staff to a more prestigious section very soon. That would mean a new lad, unskilled, untrained and with all the knife skills of a giraffe.

Any doubts he might have had about the risk he was going to take vanished and he rose and made his way to the dim kitchen. There was a little warmth from the banked up fires, but it was still cold enough to make him shiver. Being cold in the kitchen was a rare thing and would not last for long; in a very short time the bakers would be firing their brick ovens to bake the bread which had been proving overnight and they would be followed by the scullions who would begin cooking the porridge which was breakfast for the lower orders, and they would be followed by the chefs preparing the eggs, bacon, sausages and other delicacies demanded by the higher ones.

Quine took a frying pan from the rack. Normally he would have cooked something as small as this on a brazier fired with charcoal, but he did not have time for it to reach the correct cooking temperature, so he stirred the fire under the spit and wedged his pan on the hot embers.

While it warmed he considered the single mushroom he had bought to the kitchen. The other two were safely hidden away in a bag tucked into the roof of the privy where their smell was disguised. What to do? Should he slice it, dice it or fry it whole? He decided to slice it.

He thought it might ooze, the colour suggested some sort of liquid might be responsible, but when he put his knife into the blue outer skin he found the flesh beneath was pure white. He thought how lovely the slices looked, white rimmed with blue and the blush of the purple gills. He hoped the heat would not destroy the pretty picture.

Taking a lump of the best butter, he cast it into the pan and watched it fizz and foam. It was too hot, but that was the price he would have to pay for cooking on such a crude source of heat. He added the slices of mushrooms, carefully turning them in the hot fat. As he watched the butter took on the purple shade of the gills, but the blue and white of the fungus stayed. It reminded Quine of the fantastically expensive blue and white china which adorned the sideboard in the dining hall. Not even his lordship dined off those.

When he thought they had cooked enough, Quine took the pan to the table. His instinct was to add salt and pepper, but he thought it would be best to see how they tasted in their natural state.

He speared a piece with a fork and carried it to his lips.

And there it stayed, hovering in mid-air. He wanted to put it in his mouth, he wanted to know how it tasted, but he also did not want to die. On the other hand this could be his golden opportunity. He tried again, but once again his courage failed him. It was no good, he could not bring himself to eat something which might mean not only death, but an agonising death. He would throw the mushroom on the fire and that would be an end of it.

As he turned to toss the contents of the pan into the grate he caught a sudden blast of aroma. There was no way of describing it, it was not the usual smell that came from well cooked food or the delightful odour which had come from the mushroom their uncooked state. It was all of them, only a hundred times more powerful.

Saliva filled Quine's mouth and his stomach rumbled in anticipation. He *had* to eat it! He had never in his life experienced such hunger or such greed. He wanted to eat this one and the ones hanging in the privy and any more that Hurl could find for him.

The fork rushed to his lips and the warm slice was inside before he knew what he was about and his mouth was full of the taste of the wild. There were earthy tones and the suggestion of wild boar and juniper and quail, there were hints of heather honey and bilberries and chestnuts. When these passed there was an aftertaste of wild thyme and freshwater mussels. Never in his life had Quine tasted anything like it and he could hardly contain his rush to eat another piece. If this was going to kill him, it was worth it.

He looked with deep regret at the final slice. He wanted to savour this last morsel, make it last, enjoying every tiny layer of mind-blowing flavour, but the sounds of others on their way to begin work meant he had to rush it into his mouth. He had no wish to be found alone in the kitchen this early, plus he needed somewhere to go and see what reaction he might have.

Quickly he ducked into the dried goods store; it was a long narrow room with a dogleg down the end where he could wait unseen if the boys came in for porridge or the bakers for more flour. Hidden around this corner, he sank down to the floor amongst the sacks of dried beans and pulses to await developments.

To his relief and delight nothing happened, apart from a small burp which rose from his stomach and again filled his mouth with the delicious aromas. It was quiet and warm and after his succession of sleepless nights, Quine was tired and he found himself drifting. As the sounds from the kitchen began to fade and his limbs sagged into a state of wonderful relaxation, he jerked himself back to life. Was this how the blue mushroom killed, not violently with all the drama of vomiting and fits, but softly and quietly? He shook his head, trying to rid himself of the feeling of fatigue.

It passed and he thought it probably was nothing more than being tired, but there was a slight feeling of elation which was unfamiliar. There was also a tingling around his lips and cheeks. It was not painful, but it did itch a bit. The feeling spread to his nose and he had to rub it hard, which eased it, but did not stop it; then he felt as if itching had exploded over his whole face, up to his eyes and on to his forehead, across his cheeks to his ears and down his chin to his neck. It lasted barely a second, but it had been a disgusting and frightening sensation.

Quine, scared and trembling from the pain, waited for death, but death was busy elsewhere and failed to put in an appearance. For a moment he thought he had peed himself, but investigation showed he had not, although there was a definite feeling of excess heat in his groin area, but this like the itch faded very quickly.

He had definitely had a reaction, but that did not mean everyone else would. Very often the toxins in mushrooms affected only certain people, the way the chicken-of-the-woods had got the head chef. It could also have happened because he had not cooked them long enough; he would try again and this time he would leave them in the pan for longer.

What he needed now was an excuse for being in the store or the other staff would wonder what he had been doing in there, and he had a very good idea what they would come up with and he had no desire to listen to jokes on that subject. Most of what was in there were siege rations, hence their being tucked away down this obscure backwater. There were sacks and sacks of dried beans from the floor to the ceiling.

Quine studied them with chagrin. They were not food for his lordship's table, but on the other hand there were split yellow peas and these could be made into pease pudding which could be served to those below the salt and the economy of such a belly-filling dish would please the steward.

He looked over the sacks to see which had beans and which peas, and as he did so his eye caught an anomaly, something metallic and of unusual shape. He put out his hand to investigate, but instead of feeling cool steel or something similar, he encountered nothing more than hessian and beans. Puzzled, he looked again and there was definitely something there which was not beans. Cautiously he pulled away the sack to see if the object was behind, but his touch told him there was nothing there but more beans.

He shook his head and rubbed his eyes, and despite everything logic and reason told him, he could still see something. It seemed to hover in front of the sacks, a shadow or perhaps a trick of the light, and now it had been joined by two discs.

Quine removed another sack of beans and then another. As he did so the shadow objects got a little clearer and took on a more robust form. When he had removed a dozen sacks of beans, getting dustier and dustier as he went back into the heap, he found a piece of rag tied around something. Hands shaking, he untied the crude knot and found inside two small gold coins, a dozen or so copper ones and a silver nutmeg grater.

He did not know what shocked him most, the discovery or that he had "seen" it through nearly five feet of solid beans! Where had it come from and who had put such a valuable cache in here? He slipped the coins into his apron pocket. They would not be hard to explain, but the grater was another matter. He inspected it; there was still half a nutmeg inside and it had the look of a well-used personal item. Where had he heard something about a missing grater? He knew he had done so, but the memory was elusive, so he put it with the coins, replaced the hill of beans, and grabbing a bag of peas went out into the kitchen.

No-one noticed him; they were all too busy getting the first meal of the day ready. Quine poured the peas into a huge pot and added water; he would leave them to soak for a few hours before he cooked them. Still ignored by the rest of the brigade, he began his preparation. It was work his hands knew without the need of his brain, so as the mounds of finely diced and sliced vegetables grew under his knife, Quine was able to think.

There was much to occupy his thoughts — where had the grater come from, how had it got into the dry goods store and exactly how had he been able to "see" where it was? While not a great or deep thinker, even Quine was able to work out the mushroom must have played some part in his discovery. It was the only variation in his life.

Slowly from the depths of his memory an answer came to the first part of the puzzle. When he had first come to Castle Gregannor it had been rife with gossip about a couple of kitchen hands who had been summarily dismissed for theft. They had both been caught selling household food to a man who supplied the local inn. The head chef at the time had also reported the loss of a large number of gold coins and his silver gilt nutmeg grater.

He had also been dismissed when Quine had

been there less than a year for the same crime — theft, only his had been on a monumental scale, costing the household thousands. After the steward had dismissed him, his lordship had hanged him.

It appeared the man had lied about his losses; the grater was only silver and there were only two gold coins. No doubt he had hoped his lordship would replace what he *said* had gone. It was obvious someone had hidden the loot intending to return for them when the fuss died down, probably one of the hands, but their greater crime had been discovered and the chance had gone.

A smile began to stretch Quine's face. No-one was going to come looking for his find now and no-one knew about it except him. It was his to keep and a generous contribution to his running away fund.

Then another and far more intriguing thought rose up — he had not "seen" the copper coins, only the gold ones. The grater was silver, the other noble metal. Did this mean he would be able to know where treasure was concealed? This was a dangerous idea. There was always a good chance that the person who concealed wealth knew exactly where it was and would know if it disappeared, but lost treasure was another matter. He was still smiling when his two scullions finally made it into the kitchen.

They were in a very cocky mood and it was obvious they were going to be as difficult as they could be that day. Quine's contented smile threw them and took away some of their confidence, but not for long. As they larked about, dropping things and spilling water, salt and vinegar, Quine noticed something on the older one's apron. He thought it was a stain of some sort, but it was the same shape and size as a coin and he realised it was on the *inside* of the apron's pocket and he could "see" it, so it must be either silver or gold, silver by the size of it.

Quine allowed himself a cynical smile; the boy had got more for his arse than promotion the night before, he must have performed to a high standard. Did he know just how hard he was now going to have to work to maintain his advantage? Quine knew the head chef's tastes; in less than a year the boy would be too old to excite the disgusting old pederast.

Later on in the day he knew who would be taking his scullion's place. The older boy was sent off to his new station and was replaced by a frightened child of no more than thirteen. He had, as Quine knew he would, no knife skills, did not know a cabbage from a radish, and was conscious of his nakedness and kept trying to turn his back away from the gaze of the head chef and towards the table. Shorthanded and under pressure, Quine had little time to ponder all the implications of his discovery, but there was a knot of excitement in his stomach which kept tying and untying itself.

He needed to know long the effects of the mushroom would last. In an ideal world it would be permanent, but life had taught Quine nothing in this life is ever perfect and he was neither surprised nor disappointed when later in the day, he studied the steward and could not "see" the silver chain and medal all his lordship's senior staff wore under their clothes.

He would have to experiment to find out how long the effects of the mushroom lasted, also whether he would have the same reaction he had had the first time and if cooking it longer to kill the toxins meant it would not work.

All thoughts of serving the ultimate dish to his lord had long since ceased to bother him one little bit.

What he needed were more mushrooms and he only had two left. On the other hand Hurl would be back in a couple of days and he should be able to persuade him to either give him more or tell him were to find them, in the meantime he would risk another go tomorrow. He would also need to find a place where expensive items might have had been lost and overlooked.

The answer to that conundrum eluded him until bedtime, but then it came to him — the castle gardens. Not the kitchen garden, although he might on another occasion give them a look if the mushroom supply was sufficient, but the pleasure gardens where the ladies and gentlemen walked. Getting into them would not be a problem; nothing but a rustic gate and precedent stood between the gardens and the common folk, that and the knowledge any unauthorised person caught there could expect to be flogged.

Quine was not going to chance a flogging, but he was very sure he would not encounter any nobleman or woman around dawn; so the next morning, long before the birds had even uttered their first "go away, this is mine" shout, he was frying his second mushroom and gulping it down in a way its incredible flavour did not deserve. This time the itching was not as violent. Perhaps cooking it longer had been the answer, but he did experience the same rush of sensation across his face as he had before.

Stealing out of the silent kitchen and around the curtain wall to the gardens he encountered no-one except a wandering cat. It looked at him, took a second look and gave a hiss before vanishing into the shadows. The gardens were just visible in the gathering light; Quine opened the gate and slipped inside. Ahead of him was an area of contrived charm; narrow paths ran beside flower beds neatly contained by low box hedges. Every now and then there was a grass-covered hummock suitable for sitting, and in each corner there was a seat covered by a pergola where a lady and a gentleman might dally without fear of being too closely observed.

He made his way to the covered seats, arguing they were the most likely places for someone to lose a ring or a brooch and not notice the going. He was doomed to disappointment, nothing showed. Next he walked around the flower beds, taking great care to scan the area around each grassy seat again, thinking they were the obvious places for someone to mislay a coin or bit of jewellery.

He had been so confident of finding something that when he did not he cursed himself for overcooking the mushroom, however as he was making his way back to the kitchen a flash between two flagstones caught his attention. He knelt down and using his knife cut away at a heavy growth of moss; buried about two inches down was a gold tooth pick, a silly frivolous affectation lost by some fop.

Quine rubbed the dirt away from his find and

tested it with his own teeth just enough to confirm what he already knew, it really was gold. Chuckling to himself, he tucked the trinket away for safekeeping and went back to begin his day's work.

On the following day he decided to use the last mushroom, as it was beginning to show signs of deterioration. He thought about drying it for future use, but there was no guarantee its power would survive dehydration, and Hurl would be back soon. He decided not to miss the chance of adding to his increasingly heavy purse.

He was again faced with the question of where to look. There were not many places where mislaid and forgotten valuables might be lurking, especially not where Quine could go looking for them without fear of being interrupted or challenged. He decided to try the stables — ladies and gentlemen rode in and out every day and there were often visitors, any one of which could have dropped some trifle, not to mention the number of coins which were flicked to waiting grooms and ostlers. Surely some of this largesse could have slipped from fingers stiff with cold on winter mornings.

He would have to be careful with his timing; they rose early in the stables and mucking out began as soon as there was light to see. A naked light was out of the question; one spark might begin a fire and a whiff of smoke would make the horses agitated. The least sound of a distressed animal would have the lads out of the bothy as fast as a greased rat down a well larded drain pipe.

Quine invested a small amount on a good closed lantern. The soft light it provided would be enough for him to see where he was going and to "see" the tell-tale shadow of hidden wealth, but could be quickly shuttered if he had company. He had hardly begun on his stealthy progress around the yard when he spotted a coin wedged under the mounting block. It was deep in a crevice and took some time to prise it free — it turned out to be a small bit of silver. He was not sure it had been worth the broken finger nail it had cost to retrieve it, but emboldened by this early success, he continued his search.

What he found lying in a clump of creeping toadflax by the water trough made his hands shake and his eyes bulge from his head. Suddenly frightened, he thrust his find into his pocket and ran from the yard back to the kitchen as fast as he could. No-one had started work yet, but he was not prepared to risk being seen, so he scuttled into the dry goods store with his lantern and made his way to the rear.

Here he took out what he had found and examined it more closely in the light. It was a ring, a lady's ring of such magnificence he could hardly believe the evidence of his own eyes. A large square cut sapphire set in a twisting framework of gold leaves and tendrils with tiny white enamelled flowers dotted amongst the tracery. It was worth a king's ransom and possibly more dangerous than a rabid wolverine.

Quine's hands shook and he nearly dropped it. If he was found with this, he would hang. There was no way anyone could have lost this and it not be known. He was just amazed the whole castle had not been turned inside out and upside down while it was looked for. It was easy enough to keep anonymous coins and trinkets the owner did not or could not identify, but this! This was something else. What was he to do?

The first thing, he told himself, was not to panic. Whoever had lost this would be very grateful to have it returned. They would probably be so grateful they would be only too delighted to reward the honest man who had found it and wanted nothing more than to give it back to its rightful owner. This was a very pleasing thought and he began to calculate the size of reward such a piece of jewellery might command. The problem of getting it to the right person now presented itself. He would have to be careful. Many nobles, and it was obviously the property of a noble, would hang a man first and ask questions later, and there were undoubtedly any number of them who would not hesitate to lay claim to such a prize even if it was not theirs.

There was one man who could help him; he was honest and trustworthy and he had been willing to help him before. He would show his find to the steward and ask him what he should do.

\* \* \*

"Where did you get this?" the steward demanded, his eyes starting as he stared at what lay in Quine's hand.

"I found it. It was just lying in a patch of weed and I spotted it. Do you know who it belongs too?"

The steward nodded his head.

"Tell me and I'll give it back to them."

The steward grabbed his arm and dragged him into an alcove.

"You can't," he hissed. "At least, you can't do it openly."

"Why not?"

"Because my lord doesn't know it's missing."

"Doesn't know..."

"My lady lost it a month ago and she dare not tell her husband — it is an heirloom of huge importance. I've been trying to organise discreet searches without any success, but you've found it and you won't find her ungenerous, I promise you. But you must keep your mouth shut! Do you understand?"

Quine did understand and felt a glow of satisfaction; it was always good when a plan came together, especially when it looked likely to be as profitable as this one had the potential to be. It was in fact even better than Quine had hoped. The steward came to get him in the evening after dinner was over and conducted him up the back stairs to the solar.

Her ladyship was there alone, except for her lap dogs. They raised their heads as Quine entered the room and both began to growl, the hackles on their backs rising.

"Quiet, you silly animals," she said, waving a tambour frame at them. They stopped growling, but neither of them relaxed. "They don't appear to like you overmuch, cook."

Quine sank down on one knee.

"I'm sorry, my lady."

"Why? Because my dogs don't like you?"

"Um... yes," he replied, feeling foolish and out

of place in this scented bower full of rich fabrics and the fragrance of wax candles.

She laughed,

"Well there is no need for you to be sorry about that, especially as I am so deeply grateful to you. I would've been in serious disgrace if my husband had discovered the loss."

Quine could think of nothing to say, so he just nodded. She smiled again, and he thought what a nice lady she was. To his relief she had either forgotten or forgiven the business with the onion rings.

"You've no idea why, have you?" she continued. "To you this is nothing more than a pretty bauble, an expensive bauble perhaps, but nothing more."

Actually Quine thought it was a hell of a lot more than that, but he did not feel it was his place to argue with her.

"I will tell you why, because I feel you've a right to know just how great your service to me has been. This ring..."

He saw she was wearing it and as she raised her hand the blue stone flashed in the candlelight.

"... is the last known piece of the Gregannor Treasure," she continued. "We know what it was made up of, there was an inventory made in the time of my lord's great grandfather. All of it was jewellery, diamonds, rubies and pearls the size of pigeon's eggs, and all set by the hand of a master. This ring was just one of the lesser pieces, so you can imagine what the rest was like."

Quine did not think he could, but he did not say so.

"Great grandpapa had a wife who adored the

collection and wore it as often as she could, but as she got older she became more and more eccentric and started hiding pieces from everyone, including her servants. Unfortunately, when it became clear she was completely demented, she had squirrelled away the whole lot, except for this ring and a bracelet."

"Where did she put it, my lady?" Quine asked.

"That is the problem, my friend, no-one knows. People searched for years, but none of it has ever been found. I doubt if it ever will turn up. I suspect she may have tossed it in the moat or dropped it down a well or somesuch; she was little more than a babbling idiot towards the end.

So you will understand why this ring is so precious and why my husband would have been so very angry if he had discovered I had lost it."

She smiled at him and held out a velvet purse.

"Here," she said. "A reward for your honesty and extra for your silence. You won't betray me will you?"

Quine took the purse. It was delightfully weighty. "You can rely on me, my lady. I won't breathe a word."

She dismissed him with a last smile and he left the room as quickly as he could, his mind racing and reeling at what she had told him. Somewhere in the castle was a treasure so massive a man could live like a prince for the rest of his life on the proceeds, and there was no-one looking for it because they believed it was gone forever.

He had to get a fresh supply of mushrooms from Hurl.

\* \* \*

When Quine had the leisure to examine the contents of the purse he found he was richer than he had ever thought possible. What it contained, added to what he had found and his savings, amounted to three times the sum he had set as his target to leave. He did briefly consider doing just that and forgetting the inherent danger in looking for and possibly finding the treasure, but he remembered the mushrooms and while he might have second thoughts about the jewellery, the thought of once again tasting that heavenly flavour was enough to make him determined to get his hands on as many as he possibly could.

He returned to the tedium of the kitchen and tried to control his impatience with the work and instructing the new boy. This was a thankless task because once the child got over his first fears, he proved to be as clumsy as he was idle. There was no point in complaining, the brat might have been lazy, but he was not stupid and he had worked out how to manipulate the head chef within days.

Once this would have reduced Quine to a seething, writhing mass of anger and frustration, but now he just looked across the table to where the boy was reducing a magnificent cauliflower to a pile of white granules and shrugged. If that was what was acceptable to the man in charge, he was not going to argue.

Several of his dishes were returned untasted that night and the following night, but he did not care. All he could think of was Hurl's return and the possibility of mushrooms and gold.

He had assumed the young merchant would come and find him, so he was somewhat disturbed when he learnt of his return from one of the gardeners, who mentioned seeing him in passing. Throwing down his knife, Quine ran to the door, oblivious to the indignant bellow of the head chef. It was only the chill of cold air on his naked flesh which brought him to his senses.

Pleading a protesting stomach and the urgent necessity of the privy, Quine rushed to dress and, as an afterthought, collect his money from its hiding place. He found Hurl camped by the small stream on the edge of the village.

He looked up when Quine came running towards him.

"Hello," he said his wide and charming smile lighting up his face. "What brings you here?"

Quine could hardly believe his ears. When he got his breath back he wheezed "Mushrooms!" his voice coming out in a high pitched a squeak that sounded like a girl.

For a moment Hurl looked puzzled, then his brow cleared and he laughed.

"Those funny blue ones I had," he said. "You were going to find out if they were good to eat. What did you discover?"

Quine had been bothered Hurl might have tried them for himself and discovered their secret, but apparently he had not.

"They're... different," he said carefully, trying to keep his voice low and calm. "In fact, I'd like to buy all you have so I can make something a bit special for my lord."

Hurl's face fell.

"I only had a couple left," he said. "And they went all slimy, so I threw them away. I am sorry."

For a moment Quine considered throttling him, but instead he replied in a carefully controlled voice,

"That's a shame, because I would have paid you very well for them."

"You would?" Hurl said in surprise.

His face split again into his happy smile, but there was speculation in his eyes.

"I could go back to where I found them and bring the rest back if you like," he offered. "If the price is right."

"You know where they grow?" Quine said excitedly "Tell me!"

Hurl laughed.

"I will," he replied. "But not yet. I think it might be to my advantage to sell you some mushrooms now and the information later."

"How much?" Quine asked, frustration driving away all sense of caution.

The look of speculation in the young merchants eyes increased as did his smile.

"You tell me," he said.

Quine knew how much he had in his purse, he was not prepared to spend all of it, in fact he rebelled at the idea of spending anything, but getting his hands on some mushrooms very quickly was his first priority.

"I will give you a gold piece," he offered.

"Generous," Hurl said. "Very generous, but I was thinking of five pieces."

"Five!" Quine howled.

Hurl howled with laughter.

"You rise quicker to the bait than my wife," he said, still laughing. "I was joking, but I think you might make it two pieces."

Quine tried to grin back at the young man, but it was hard work. He handed over the required coins, trying to make as much of a joke about it as he could.

"When can I have them?" he asked.

"Tomorrow," Hurl replied. "Or the day after, it depends on how long it takes me to find the place again."

"So it is near," Quine said eagerly.

"Oh yes," Hurl said cheerfully. "It won't take long once I see the right landmark. To be honest, I didn't pay much attention."

"Remember I will pay for that knowledge," Quine told him. "But you won't get the money until I see where they are growing."

Hurl lost a little of his cheerful and winning demeanour.

"I'm no thief," he said coldly. "I will sell you the location, but not until you have seen exactly where they grow. You will forgive my hard negotiating, but I have a living to make and opportunities are not always easily come by."

Quine flushed with embarrassment. He was going to be rich beyond the dreams of avarice and it was a little ungracious of him to try and deprive the person who was unwittingly going to assist in the process of a little of the largesse.

"I apologise," he said gruffly. "Here is a little extra for your journey."

He handed Hurl a silver coin and was rewarded by another of the young man's charming smiles.

* * *

They arranged to meet beside the stream in two days. Quine could hardly contain himself; excitement kept coming over him in waves, he felt as if hot water was being flooded through him and his mouth was very dry all the time.

He was at the meeting place long before there was any sign of Hurl and by the time he and his wagon did appear Quine was nearly dancing with impatience.

"Hello! Hello!" Hurl called cheerfully from the seat of the wagon. "I've got them!"

Quine wanted to scream at him to keep his mouth shut, but then he wondered why because no-one else knew the secret they held and very few people would have chanced eating such a strange fungus.

Even before he got down from the wagon Hurl leaned forward and handed a wicker basket to Quine. He took it eagerly, and flicking back the piece of sacking cover, gazed down at a pile of beautiful blue mushrooms. The aroma surged up to meet his nostrils, saliva rushed into his mouth and he felt faint.

On closer inspection he was disappointed to find there were not as many as he had hoped and the majority were small, half the size of the three original ones.

"I know," Hurl said when challenged on this. "But they were all that were worth picking. There were plenty of new ones showing, but they were really tiny. I thought it best to let them grow on and let you harvest them when you are ready. Did I do right?"

Quine was quick to reassure him.

"I think they probably need about a week before the first ones will be worth taking," Hurl continued. "I'm no expert on how these things grow, but I tell you what, I've got business a few miles down the way, a gentleman needs some mace and some cloves. He's an irascible old git with no patience, but a good customer. It will take me about a week to go and pander to his demands, but when I come back I can take you to where they are growing and you can pick what you like."

Quine had a vision of a continuous harvest, or at least have enough to dry to keep him going. He wondered if he could transplant them to somewhere only he knew about. It would depend on the growing medium of course. He was no gardener, but he thought it might be possible.

"And you can pay me my money then." Hurl finished, with another of his smiles.

"I will." Quine assured him. "I'll meet you back here."

He gathered up his basket and its precious contents and prepared to go, but Hurl stopped him.

"You're not going already, are you? I thought we might have some tea. I could show you some of my other spices. I've got cardamom, both the black and the green. And green peppercorns."

"Another time," Quine muttered, desperate to get away and begin his search of Castle Gregannor, as well as eating one of the mushrooms which were tantalising his taste buds.

Once he was alone, Quine counted the contents of the basket. There were two large ones, three a little smaller, four no bigger than a normal button mushroom and a lot of really tiny ones about the size of cherries. He sorted them carefully and thought he had enough for seven days if he divided them up carefully. By the time they were gone Hurl would be back to take him to the source, and in the meantime he had seven nights to make a search of the castle.

\* \* \*

Searching something as big as a castle without anyone noticing was not an easy task and required some thought and planning. Quine had done a little discreet research and discovered there had been some major modernisation when his lordship's great grandmother had come to Gregannor as a bride. Several apartments had been created and wainscoted at enormous expense. A number of new fireplaces had also been added at the same time, together with some more practical improvements like some cupboards for storing linens.

These linen stores were the first place Quine chose to look. If he was caught, he could say he was checking on tablecloths and napkins. Why he should be doing it and not the housekeeper could be explained by his being kitchen staff.

He expended two mushrooms and two nights sleep on them, but all he found was half a ring which some girl or boy had divided as a token when they parted. Evidently one of them had lost their half and he did wonder what had been the outcome of this love affair, but only briefly.

Not unsurprisingly his daytime work suffered

as a result of his nocturnal activities, but he was able to listen to the screaming reprimand from the head chef with total indifference. He could make as much noise as he liked. When Quine was rich enough, he was going to pay someone to slit the bastard's throat.

Sleep was in fact becoming less and less of an issue. He no longer seemed to need it and he noticed the itching sensation he had previously experienced when he ate the blue mushrooms had receded to nothing more than a slight irritation around his nasal passages and the corners of his eyes.

He had more luck when he began to look at the fireplaces; it was not yet cold enough for fires to be lit in every room, so he could look into each without fear of burning himself. He was rewarded with a gold bead which must have once been part of the adornment of a lavish dress and a heavy silver charm in the form of an eye. He took this to be a sign of good luck and began to carry it in a bag around his neck.

Once or twice on his nightly perambulations he thought he had company, but he never saw anyone and was inclined to think it was just his imagination playing tricks on him.

By now his store of mushrooms was getting very low. He had meant to ration himself very carefully, but the scent which greeted him every time he went to the basket was so intoxicating he had been tempted into slip some of the tiny ones into his mouth uncooked.

The uncooked state brought back the itching sensation, but it also sharpened his "vision". It was on the fifth night, having succumbed to temptation very badly and eating three of the smallest mushrooms raw, that he made his great discovery.

As he walked through one of the disused apartments, looking at the carved panelling, he "saw" the telltale shadow of metal behind one of them, a lot of metal.

He was so excited he nearly stopped breathing. He had found it, the secret treasure of Castle Gregannor or at the very least another unknown cache. Staring hard at the panel, he saw the bundle was about the size of a large melon. He could not make out individual shapes, but whatever was behind the wood was definitely silver or gold. He was fairly sure it was gold. Lately he had begun to notice a difference between the two metals — gold seemed to be denser to his fungus-enhanced sight.

Having the gift of knowing there was something hidden behind the wood was one thing; getting it out without leaving a trace was another. Quine ran his fingers all over the panel and all the way around it, but he could not discover any secret latch or lever no matter how hard he looked. He looked, for hours and hours, only giving up when dawn broke and there was the risk of being found by a punctual maid. Reluctantly he went to begin his work in the kitchen, seething with frustration.

When Quine got ready to resume the following night he reached automatically for the basket of mushrooms. By now there were only four small ones left. If he ate them raw they would last for the next two nights, but after that there would be no more until Hurl lead him to where they grew.

It was only as he was chewing one and thinking

again how wonderful it tasted that it crossed his mind he did not need them anymore. He had found what he was looking for. He knew he ought to put the second one back and start to dry it with the others for the future, but when he tried to return it to the basket he found he was very reluctant to do so. It was the taste and the smell; it was so beguiling, and despite his good intentions, he could not resist the pull of the fungus and quickly gobbled it down.

As he made his silent way back to the wainscoted room he thought long and lovingly about what he had found. Tonight he would have the leisure to examine every nook, cranny and knob; surely he would find the trigger. After all, a batty old lady had been able to find it again and again.

The room was in deep darkness when he entered, darker than it had been the night before. He opened the cover of his lantern just a crack and saw some heavy curtains had been hung over the window so no moon or starlight could penetrate. This bothered him for a moment, but then he remembered winter was coming and soon all the windows would be covered and thick tapestries would be hung on the walls to try and combat the chill of the season.

He had examined every part of the wall where his panel stood, so logic suggested the catch must be on one of the others. He moved towards the one opposite and then stopped. All the hairs on the back of his neck rose and he stood stock still — he was not alone. There was not a sound in the room, not a hint of someone breathing or so much as a tiny rustle of clothing, but he knew he was not alone.

Slowly, very slowly, he turned, allowing just a hint of light to show. Over by the fireplace was a patch of deeper darkness. It was unmoving, but Quine's "eye" saw the shadow of hidden metal in the middle. For one dreadful second he thought it was a dagger, but it looked like silver and the mass was not consistent with a weapon. It looked more like a chain and medal.

Fingers trembling, Quine opened the door of the lantern a little more and illuminated the face of the steward. He sighed with relief; here was a friend and one who would listen to his excuses with a sympathetic ear.

"Um... you startled me, sir," he said weakly for want of something better to say.

"Did I?" the steward replied. "You didn't surprise me. Open the lantern all the way."

Because he did not feel he had very much choice, Quine did as he was told and as the light flooded the apartment he beheld a sight so terrible his eyes bulged from his head, the blood roared in his ears and he thought he was going to vomit.

Someone had taken an axe to the panelling and reduced it to splinters. The destruction had revealed a small black recess and Quine did not need his gift to show him it was completely empty of any gold or silver.

He turned to the steward, his hand clenching into a fist and vitriol spitting from his mouth. All that stopped him from murdering the small man was the cocked pistol levelled in his direction.

"You followed me," Quine hissed in accusation.

"Certainly not," the steward replied. "I've better things to do with my time. One of the stable boys did that. They are rather small and good at not being noticed."

"Where is it?" Quine demanded, this being the thing now uppermost in his mind.

"It's with my lady of course," the steward replied. "I have to say when she first proposed this plan I was very cynical, but she insisted she had heard stories about this mushroom which helped people see in the dark. For some reason I thought that was more to do with carrots, but she was adamant she had seen or read something about it. It was all those mushroom dishes you kept presenting which brought it to mind."

Quine could only gape at him in horror.

"Hurl?" he gasped.

"The young merchant? He said he could get hold of some. As I said, I had no faith whatsoever in the whole idea, but when you found the ring she had laid ready for you, I must say I was convinced."

"Was... was there treasure?" For some reason Quine had to know.

"Good God, yes! I've never seen the like. When the men broke the panelling down they hauled out such stuff. I could hardly bring myself to believe the pearls were real, they were so big."

He looked at the broken panel and sighed.

"That is going to take some repairing. The catch is on the other side of the room — there was a cord running from one side to the other. If it's any consolation you wouldn't have got it open even if you'd found it. Rats had eaten through the string."

It was not a consolation.

"Anyway," the steward continued. "My lady is delighted and my lord even more so, so the loss of a bit of wood need not concern us."

His face hardened.

"You will, of course, be gone by morning. My lady says you'll be allowed to keep what you found and what she gave you, but you're no longer employed here and if I or anyone else sees you much after daybreak you will be flogged and then sent packing."

Perhaps it was the stricken look on Quine's face which softened his expression.

"You know it is always best to stick at what you are good at," the steward said. "You're an excellent cook and what you serve has always been appreciated. It is the way of the world that the ordinary everyday things don't get the acclaim they deserve, but that doesn't mean they aren't recognised."

He patted Quine's shoulder.

"Make sure you're gone, I would be most upset if I had to order you to be flogged."

With this valediction he strolled out of the room, leaving Quine to his misery. He stood for a while racked by silent sobs while his world and his plans lay shattered all around him.

What was he going to do now? What did he have to make a new life with?

There was the remaining money of course, and the small trinkets he had found, they were worth a bit. It was enough to set his feet on the road to a new place where he could start again. And he still had his mushrooms; they would give him the ability to find more.

An idea began to form in his head. Hurl might have supplied the mushrooms, but it was obvious he had no idea what they could do; if he had he would never have parted with them or been willing to sell more to Quine.

There was now no reason to keep the secret from the man. Together they could make a fortune and they could do it honestly, offering their services to people who had lost valuables. He did not need the Gregannor jewels; the two of them could find better and bigger rewards. Hurl would supply the mushrooms and Quine the "sight".

He thought of Hurl with his open honest face and charming smile. The boy was no fool and he drove a hard bargain, but he was just the sort of person to go into partnership with. He even knew his way to all the best houses, the sort of places where rich people mislaid rich objects.

This was where his future lay. He would shake the dust of the castle from his feet this very day and be waiting for Hurl when he got back. Once he had revealed the secret to him the two of them could go and pick the rest of the crop, and then the world would be their oyster.

\* \* \*

Gathering what little he had in the way of possessions and making sure he had his last few mushrooms, Quine left Castle Gregannor well before dawn. He strode out in the crisp morning air in a very cheerful frame of mind. He might have missed one fortune, but there were others out there. For one moment as the high chimneys and battlements dipped out of sight he had a moment of regret, but he reflected if this had not happened, he would have just gone on year after year getting more and more unhappy. In more ways than one this had been a blessing. He was free, he had coin enough to live on, more than enough as he would now not have to pay Hurl. Without thinking, he tossed a mushroom into his mouth and allowed the glorious flavour to fill it and slip down to his welcoming stomach. There had been a setback, but everything was going to be good from now on.

And that is exactly what he told Hurl the following day when he met up with him in the field by the stream. The young man listened to all he had to say with his mouth open.

"You are telling me that those mushrooms have got some sort of special powers?"

"Yes," Quine replied, laughing with joy.

"I will admit I was a bit puzzled when they were ordered and it took me a long time to find a source of them. I was even more surprised when they told me only to show them to the kitchen staff. I really didn't want to do it, I was frightened they might kill someone, but you seemed to know what you were talking about, so I let you have a few. As you know, I threw the rest away, they kept worrying me."

"Someone else knows where they grow?" Quine said, ignoring most of this and fixing on the part which worried him.

"Yes and no," Hurl replied. "I found a reference to them in an herbal and I went looking in the places it said they grew. It was a very old book and a bit mildewed in places, so I was lucky to be able to make it out."

"Have you still got the book?"

"It's in the back of the wagon somewhere," Hurl replied. "Look here, Quine, I'm sorry, but I think I'm going to need proof of all this. It all seems a bit far-fetched to me."

"I know it's hard to believe," Quine replied. "But it's all true."

At Hurl's insistence they set up a series of tests, but it was only after Quine had found, and identified as silver, a dozen coins hidden in a dozen places, including under rocks that Hurl shook his head in amazed delight.

"This is fantastic. You're right; we're going to make *so much* money."

Quine nodded in eager agreement.

"All we need are the mushrooms. If we can get to them tonight we could be on our way tomorrow. Where should we start, a city maybe?"

Quine longed to see a city.

As they and the wagon jolted along the road Hurl talked of options and Quine listened in deep contentment, and without thinking ate the last of his mushrooms.

Hurl looked at him curiously.

"Do they taste good?" he asked.

Quine froze; he had no wish to share either his new ability or the mushrooms.

"Not really," he lied. "They need to be cooked to make them taste all right. I've been lucky, I haven't had a toxic reaction, but they could be very dangerous to someone else."

"I see," Hurl replied and Quine began to wish he had stopped by the kitchen to collect his knives.

They rode on in silence, the road leading them

through a steep valley slotted with deep ravines. It was a lonely place, the sort of place were a man could die and his body never be found. Hurl halted the wagon in what seemed to be a totally random spot.

"Why have we stopped?" Quine asked as Hurl secured the reins and put feed bags on the mules' noses.

"We've come to collect mushrooms," Hurl said in surprise. "They grow in the cave up there."

He pointed to a dark opening above them.

Quine was now nervous and highly suspicious; he was very unwilling to enter the cave unarmed.

"You go and get them," he said.

Hurl gave him a look wounded sorrow; there was even the suggestion of tears in his eyes.

"I thought we were going to be partners," he said, his voice cracking. "Possibly even friends, however, if you believe I'm going to attack you in the cave and eat the mushrooms myself, I think it might be best if we part ways. I'll go and gather what you want and drop you at the next village."

Quine squirmed with guilt and dread. He had always been part of a large brigade in the kitchens and while he might not have liked everyone, he was at least never alone. Here in this desolate spot he understood how awful loneliness could be and he feared it. He had also hurt this man, who had nothing but their best interests at heart.

"Let's go together," he said, holding out his hand in mute apology.

Hurl smiled his wide, warm smile and shook the offered hand with a firm, friendly grip.

They walked up to the cave entrance side by side. Hurl lit a candle and they made their way into the cool dampness. Quine looked eagerly around and was rewarded by the sight of blue mushrooms growing upon a low hump white with the thick tracery of mycelium.

He ran forward, crooning with delight. There were dozens of them, some huge, far bigger than anything he had seen before. He gently broke one of the giants away from its fruiting mound and cradled it in his hand. It was nearly as big as a bread roll and the smell was overpowering. He did not even try to control himself; he sank his teeth in and took an enormous satisfying bite. It was *so* good; so much better than the small one. He knew he had made a mistake eating them young, they needed to mature.

"Good?" Hurl asked, from where he was standing in the opening.

"Oh yes," Quine replied and took another bite.

"Have you still got the itching?"

"No," Quine said. "That went off."

"Excellent. How about the thirst?"

It occurred to Quine that he had not been thirsty for a couple of days; in fact he could not remember the last time he had taken a drink.

"Why do you ask?"

"I just wanted to see how far along you were," Hurl replied.

Quine took another bite of his mushroom. "What do you mean?"

Hurl gave him his charming smile.

"Well," he said. "This one is nearly exhausted and I like to know that my supply is not going to run out."

Quine turned back to the white mound and it

seemed to him it bore a strong resemblance to a corpse. A closer look proved the resemblance to be all too real. Up the far end where dozens of tiny mushrooms clustered were the two blackened eye sockets of a skull. The mushroom he was eating sagged in his nerveless fingers, but he did not entirely release his weakened grip.

"I've tried growing them on all sorts of things," Hurl said. "But nothing really works as well as a fresh body which has been impregnated with the spores from the inside.

I must say you've proved to be an excellent choice. Sometimes morality gets in the way of venality and I'm forced to take drastic action, but you, my friend, were more than happy to keep on eating my little darlings."

"You knew?" Quine gasped.

"Oh yes. Trading would provide me with an adequate income, but these things are making me rich, very rich."

Quine was finding thought elusive, but some of this got through.

"How?"

Hurl tutted at such denseness.

"Surely that's obvious even to you. On my travels I visit any number of places where things of value have been lost over the years. You would be amazed at what ploughmen turn up in a field. It's not hard to introduce one of my blues to someone. If they're wary of eating them, as they often are, they are usually quite happy to take them dried and powdered.

I am always delighted by how willing the ignorant are to ingest anything they believe to be an aphrodisiac."

He chuckled to himself.

"Of course, when they discover what effect it is really having they're always very eager to get their hands on more. Just like you, my friend. And they will pay me with everything they find to be able to get more."

Again his wide smile spread across his face as he watched Quine struggle to comprehend all of this.

"I expect you're wondering why the world is not covered in corpses growing blue mushrooms?"

Quine, who was trying to decide between two mushrooms of equal size, nodded his head and this made Hurl laugh.

"Of course you are," he said, grinning. "The one near the groin is the biggest. As I was saying, they don't litter the world because I don't allow them to do so. I don't allow anyone to eat enough to start cropping when they expire. Did I mention that death is inevitable right from the first bite? How very remiss of me."

Somewhere deep inside a part of Quine cried out in anguish and despair, but it was a part he no longer had the power to hear.

"I've no idea how her ladyship found out about me, but she did and she was very generous. At least I thought she was very generous at the time. I've since found out the value of what she wanted you to find and I think now she was somewhat mean, the cunning minx."

This mention of the events of the day before did get past the fumes in Quine's brain.

"She trapped me?"

Hurl considered this.

"I think you trapped yourself," he said. "I helped of course, but you could have told her what you could do when you found her ring, but you chose not to. Far more importantly, you could have told me what we might have shared... well, not shared, because you're going to die, but you stopped me getting my hands on a fortune and that was when I decided you should make up for it by supplying me with my next crop."

"I'm leaving," Quine announced, lurching to his feet.

"No you're not," Hurl replied confidently. "You don't want to leave."

"Yes I do," Quine slurred in retort, but as he did so he sprayed the ground with the mouthful of mushroom he was eating.

He wanted to leave and he tried to do so, but the smell pulled him back. He would go, but not until he had enjoyed one last taste, He had already picked and eaten the biggest he could see and he wept to think that it was gone and he could not eat it again, but near where the ribs had been was one nearly as big and once he had finished it he knew he would have had enough and be able to walk away.

Hurl was no longer in the cave which was good; there was no-one who might want to share. He would just eat one more and then he would pick the rest to take away with him. There was a world full of lost treasure out there and he could find it. He did not need Hurl, all he needed were these wonderful mushrooms which tasted so marvellous.

Perhaps he would have just one more before he left.

# ABOUT THE AUTHOR

*Bev Allen is married and mother of two adult children...*
Or, Bev is a crazy old woman who writes weird short stories about things like a bloke having sex with his garden pond and, when she has remembered her medication, sci-fi/fantasy adventures liberally laced with soldiers. She has a fondness for soldiers, which should not be taken to mean she stands on street corners in garrison towns.

You can find her on Facebook here
https://www.facebook.com/bev.allen.940
And Twitter here
https://twitter.com/BevAllen23
And you can follow her on her blog here
https://kentishmaid.wordpress.com/


Other books by Bev Allen include:

## JABIN
A novel stuffed full of soldiers. Not bothered by soldiers? You're stronger than me, I have trouble

resisting a uniform... never mind, you will find destitute orphans, beautiful slave girls, dastardly pirates and a light dusting of royalty, clergy and repellent relatives. It's sci-fi folks, just not as you expect it

## THE TATTOOED TRIBES
No soldiers this time (sobs quietly), but a forest world full of tattooed tribesmen and tribal custom. Add hero No.1, an eco warrior, woodsman and diplomat, and mix with hero No.2, a teenage boy with all the sense you would expect from a hormone-raddled brain and a conviction the rules don't apply to him. There's assorted villains as well, where would an adventure story be without them?

## THE LORD OF THE FARAN HILLS
When Aulay Fitzgellis allowed himself to be talked into rebellion against his brother, the king, it never crossed his mind he might not win.
Now the only thing keeping his head on his shoulders is the leader of the mercenaries who defeated him.
Lord Darach of the Faran Hills is willing to save Aulay, but he also has other things on his mind; the possibilities of a new type of weapon called a "musket" and how to stop his bagpipers assaulting his ears.

All three titles will be published by Cathaven Press in print and new ebook versions later in 2022/3.

Printed in Great Britain
by Amazon